THE VERY FIRST TIME

The Very First Time

RICHARD FISHER

Doubleday & Company, Inc., Garden City, N.Y., 1959

All of the characters in this book are fictitious, and any resemblance to actual persons, living or dead, is purely coincidental.

LIBRARY OF CONGRESS CATALOG CARD NUMBER 59–6354

PRINTED IN THE UNITED STATES OF AMERICA
FIRST EDITION

To my Father and Mother

THE VERY FIRST TIME

1

What a crazy guy he was. Robert Garrety, I mean. When he invited me to a swimming party that day in early August, I should have known better, remembering what had happened a year ago. I had been in eighth grade then, a senior in grammar school, and he was only in the scummy seventh, so we didn't communicate too much. In fact, he didn't even like me, and he said things like "Hello, zit on wheels." But he was too insignificant to worry over. Then one warm, smoggy spring afternoon he suggested a swim in the pool of a "friend."

There were four of us. He led us on our bikes up a steep mountain canyon to a dense woodland estate, a huge place, wild and overgrown with mountain brush. We climbed a flight of stone stairs to a garden terrace, and discovered the pool. It was hewn out of shale, like a rock cavern, and the water was glassy green with plants floating in it; a tunnel at one end led to a second section. Except for ourselves, there was no one in sight.

"The pool looks pretty dirty," I said.

"No, it doesn't!" he contradicted. "It's always like that."

"What about the owner?"

"It's all right, I tell you. I can come in any time!"

We swam for about twenty minutes. Then a short, pudgy man in a bathrobe appeared with a butler and asked what the hell we were doing.

Robert got out of the pool. "Don't you remember me? I came here once with Mike Jason, sir."

The short man nodded reluctantly. "Well, Mike's father is a friend of mine. And Mike can bring anybody he wants. But I think you boys had better go now."

Later, Robert insisted he had done us a great favor in leading us two or three miles to swim for twenty minutes in a dirty pool before being thrown out; we didn't quite agree with him. He never tried to become accepted by us upper classmen again.

However, he had changed a lot since the old days, and in fact when we ran across each other in a drugstore, I scarcely recognized him. He was almost as tall as I was, short by an inch or so, and he wore a white dress shirt rolled over twice at the cuff, like I did, levis with a thin roll on the bottom, and loafers. He had light brown hair combed long at the sides and a straight, noble-looking nose that wasn't too big for his face any more so that his eyes had come to dominate it—large, dark eyes that reminded you of a cat's.

"Hi, Jack," he'd said. "You go to St. Francis High now, don't you?"

I said I did, that I was a sophomore providing I made up my freshman algebra credit in summer school. "I have a two-hour class every day," I told him. "Ten to twelve."

"Is it pretty tough? St. Francis, I mean."

"Somewhat."

"I might go there this September."

I was a little surprised, as Garrety had never impressed me as being much of a brain. Not that I am, myself, exactly; but I have what they call a retentive mind—in everything except algebra. St. Francis accepts only two hundred freshmen each year and since five or six hundred boys apply for admission, they have a stiff entrance exam. The two hundred with the highest marks are chosen and the next fifty placed on the waiting list. Garrety was probably one of these, I decided.

"Hope you make it," I said. I was sure he would fail.

"Oh, I made it. I came in twenty-fifth on the tests. What was your score last year?"

"Seventieth." I had been seventy-third.

"It's just," he went on, "that my father keeps hinting about public schools being free and how we have the best in the country right here in L.A."

He kept popping up after that, usually waiting in the school parking lot at noon when class broke up. I tried to brush him off at first, but he got along well with my friends, holding his own, and my opinion of him grew higher.

So when he asked me to this barbecue-swim party at the home of some girl named Ellie, I said okay. But I should have known better.

"You'll like Ellie," he said. "I have to go home for my trunks and I can loan you a pair. Then we'll drive over in my mother's brand-new Buick. Everyone will be crushed as the new car comes charging."

It was hot and the town baked under the bright August sun. We walked to his house and he let us in with a key he got under the doormat. It was one story, white stucco, with a Spanish tile roof and an unfruitful banana tree near the front door. Inside everything was spotless and well kept, all the curtains drawn against the sunlight. No one else seemed to be there.

"You sure it's all right to take the car?" I asked.

"Sure," he said.

"You know how to drive?"

"Of course! Don't have fears."

I sat in his room while he changed. The desk was cluttered with World War II ammunition shells, pencils, cuff-links, and pennies. There was a picture of a blond woman on the bureau with cat eyes and a faint, charming smile. I couldn't read the inscription in the dusk of the room. He came over quickly and put it in a drawer.

"Is that your mother?"

He nodded. "She lives back East. She's an actress."

"Oh."

He reached into a drawer, and threw a small, framed photograph over to me. "My sister."

She was three or four years old.

"Is she back East, too?"

"Yes." He took out a few more. "Here's my false father." He was a slim, dark-haired man with pockets of shadow in his eyes, standing against the side of a building. "Now here's true father and false mother." His young stepmother had a hawklike, handsome face and shoulder-length hair. The man beside her was tall and robust.

"You don't look much like your father," I said.

"I don't, do I?" He slipped his pants back on over his trunks. "Let's go."

We went out into the driveway, and he started the car. "You sure it's all right?" I asked again.

He nodded, and backed the car into the street; then he put his foot on the brake and looked over at me. "You know how to drive, don't you, Jack?"

"No," I said, "I don't know how to drive."

He looked at me a second longer, and the engine went dead. He started it again, went into reverse, and we zoomed backward. He cut the wheel quickly, and then slammed on the brakes. At least we were facing the right direction.

"Garrety, you sure *you* know how to drive?"

He nodded and sped forward, with the wheel slipping away from him. We swerved to a halt at a boulevard stop, and the engine died again.

"Shouldn't I get out?"

"No!" He made a right-hand turn on the railroad crossing, and I relaxed a little. Then he went into a right on a two-lane street and, rounding the curve, the car surged forward with terrific speed. Out of the corner of my eye I could see the wheel slipping away from him again.

"Watch it!" I yelled. I was looking at a utility pole on the sidewalk, and as I looked, we jumped the curb and rammed our fender into it. I was speechless. *This little idiot,* I thought. The windshield was cracked and shivered in places; there was a numbness in my shoulder. I opened the door and got out. My knees began shaking, and I felt a chill go through me. Robert got out and studied the car.

I wandered up to a drugstore and wandered back. Somebody pointed out that my shirt was bloody. Police officers took us up to the emergency hospital where glass was removed from my shoulder and the wound was stitched up. We answered questions, and Robert admitted he had taken the car without permission, and that—and it seemed disgraceful and shocking to me—he was just going on fourteen.

"Jack!" he said. "Quite a nice time we had, wasn't it?"

I didn't smile back. An account was published in the local newspaper, which later served as a weird kind of esteem.

I went home on the bus and got off with a terrific headache. I spent the next three days in bed, and vowed I would never have anything more to do with Garrety. Shortly afterwards we moved several miles deeper into Los Angeles, and I stopped going to summer school, satisfied I could pass a re-examination in algebra at St. Francis. I no longer lived in Robert's community, and the possibility wasn't high I'd even see him at prep school this fall. It got to look like about the easiest vow I ever kept.

2

There were a thousand boys at St. Francis, twenty-five class rooms, thirty-one teachers, R.O.T.C., me, and Robert. The first time I found out about Robert was at noontime on a day in late October when I went into the crowded cafeteria and found two hundred people ahead of me before the cook had even begun to serve the food, and it was Robert who was first in line. "Jack!" he called out, like the friend he never was. But I pushed my way over to him and instructed him to buy my lunch, and five minutes later we were sitting down together, and I had broken my vow without even realizing it.

We somehow avoided the subject of the car accident. "Well, I found out you moved," he said.

"That's right."

"Where're you living now?"

I told him. "It's not bad. I kinda miss the old neighborhood, though. How do you like St. Francis?"

"I'm being thrown out."

"Who said so?" I asked, surprised.

"Mr. Raybourne hinted."

Mr. Raybourne was an English teacher, and I'd had him last year. He was young and eager and would have been successful at keeping order, maybe, in a coed class—though that is not asking much. With a bunch of boys—especially unsifted freshmen (a third of them would be gone by their sophomore year)—he appeared too simple and kind, and when it came to discipline, indecisive. "We used to riot under him," I said. "And then my mother met him on Parents Night and thought he was brilliant and that I should have respect."

He thought it over. "I don't think he's so brilliant—he don't have any sense of humor. Just listen to what happened today."

Mr. Raybourne had been a few minutes late commuting between classrooms after the period bell. While the class waited, someone decided to write on the board, "The black spot for Norman!" and beneath it Robert scrawled, "Norman—Dies at Midnight!" Then eight unsigned notes, each bearing a black spot or a dagger dripping blood, were hastily heaped on his desk.

The class was reading *Treasure Island.*

As Mr. Raybourne opened the door, a paper plane with "Death" written on it was launched from the back of the room.

Norman Raybourne shut the door, opened his mouth to say something, and caught sight of the plane. "Death" smashed into the wall and drifted down to the floor. "Who threw that?" he demanded. But then he noticed the messages on the board, dropped the subject of the plane, and made a few obliterating sweeps with the eraser. A second later he tightened his cincture, as if girding for battle, and faced the class with determination. He was a young scholastic, who in a few years would be consecrated a Catholic priest—if he lasted. He had dry brown hair, and prominent nose, eyes, and lips; he spoke with a bad lisp and his features had grown gaunt, ravaged after his first year of teaching.

"This has got to stop! I've warned you, and you've paid no attention. So now you may open your year books to page sixty-one!"

There were forty-three questions on page sixty-one.

"Homework!" The class moaned.

"Just for that, you can turn to page seventy-eight!"

"No, no," the class president interrupted, "that's enough, Mr. Raybourne."

"Page seventy-eight," Mr. Raybourne repeated. Then he stopped to answer several questions about the previous homework, and while he was speaking, patiently covering all details, too many arms began jabbing into the air and his name began being called too many times for anyone to be serious.

Finally he said, "Shut up!" and went over to his desk. A wave of pennies rolled his way. He wheeled, stared at the class balefully until the tribute had ceased, and sat down. The black spot notes were stacked neatly in front of him. He looked at them for a moment, then slowly picked one up, opened it. The color drained from his face. He opened a second note, then a third. Then he swept them all together, crushed them in his fist, and tossed the wad into the waste basket.

"Very amusing," he said, but his voice trembled. "Davis, diagram sentence eighteen on page fifty-four."

Tom Davis, the class president, walked up to the board and began making the diagram. Mr. Raybourne watched, nodding in approval, apparently oblivious to the hubbub behind him, but when Robert dropped a pencil and grunted loudly as he bent over to pick it up, he came out of his sad-eyed dream abruptly.

"Garrety!"

"Huh?"

"Get up here!"

"I didn't do anything, Mr. Raybourne!"

"I didn't say you did anything, Garrety. I just want you to finish the sentence."

Robert stared at the board. "I don't get all those little lines," he said.

There was laughter.

"Make a stab at it."

He made a stab, and Mr. Raybourne marked him down for zero. "Pray to the Lord for wisdom," he said humorously, feeling his way back out of his early despair.

"'Lujah, 'Lujah!" said a troublemaker, and the class burst out laughing.

Tears flashed suddenly in Mr. Raybourne's eyes. "You boys," he said, shaking his head slowly—"*you boys are going to burn on the frying rock!*"

The class roared. Mr. Raybourne turned a deep red. He wheeled desperately on Robert, who was laughing hysterically. "I'm marking you for F. Sit down."

"But, Mr. Raybourne——"

"You can stay for detention, too. Sit down."

"Mr. Raybourne——"

"Sit down!" He raised his book and rushed at him.

The class broke into new laughter.

Robert scurried back to his desk, sat down, and let out a sigh. He should have known better than to laugh.

Things calmed down a little after that. But toward the end of the period, the oral questions got out of control again.

"Those," Mr. Raybourne shouted, "who don't like the way I'm teaching the class can just *get out!*"

Robert thought of the zero, the F, and the detention he had earned, then got to his feet and went to the door. Mr. Raybourne stood there stolidly in front of the class, ignoring him. Robert stepped into the empty hallway with a scared feeling, but a minute later five of his classmates followed him out. Good, Robert thought. Mr. Raybourne would not report so many to the office because of the disgrace.

As a parting gesture, they stacked a trash barrel against the door, and when Mr. Raybourne opened it, after the noon bell had rung and they were long gone, the barrel crashed down the hallway and was heard all over the building.

"See what I'm getting at?" Robert asked. "Just no sense of humor. He thinks he doesn't have to prove anything."

"I get what you mean. He thinks he doesn't have to *work* for a good class. Somebody like Father Kelly, he won't let you get away with anything. And if you ever tried, he'd just have the whole class stay after school, and that would be the end of anybody messing around."

"But if Mr. Raybourne told us to stay after school, we'd talk him out of it in five minutes."

We had finished our sandwiches and hot dogs, and were working on our half pints of milk. "Raybourne won't have you thrown out, though," I said; "they don't do that till the end of the year."

He seemed a little disappointed. After he finished his milk, he leaned forward, then hesitated. "So what girl're you going with?"

I had never discussed with him any girl I really liked, and I knew he was getting at something. "No girl. I don't have a girl."

"What about Kathy?"

I was surprised that he knew. "I stopped going with her a year ago!"

"What do you think of her younger sister, Carol?"

"She's all right, I guess."

He stole some potato chips off my plate. "She's always calling me up and inviting me places and I never go because she's ugly. I guess she likes me, though."

"Yeah?" It depressed me a little that he knew Kathy even if only through her sister. She attended a private non-coeducational school and ran around with a combination of a rich set, and a young-gentlemen set, which I used to be in until I broke off with her and was thrown out for not being polite to some parent. Our break-up really came when she grew an inch taller than I—there seemed no reason in the world why I should ever catch up with her. We parted in a sequence of abysmal neglect, but I held no conscious resentment. There was a curious aftermath. In summer school, exposed to coeds again after a two-semester fast, I became infatuated with a rather plain-looking, magnetic girl one year older and two inches taller than I. Of course, I never told anybody, and I never said a word to her. But she knew. I knew she knew. We liked what we couldn't get. It was one of the most ridiculous things that ever happened to me.

"Why do you want my opinion of Kathy's sister if you think she's ugly, which she isn't quite."

"Forget it. But tell me if Kathy sent you an invitation?"

"Invitation to what?"

"May we be beaten!"

I leaned forward. "Why? How come?"

He laughed a little harder. "She's having a big party. Everyone's been invited. And her sister invited me."

"Oh." I was embarrassed. "Listen, last year when she had a party she had *me* invite all the boys, and that was how she got her guest list!"

We spent the noon hour checking on the boys who had been invited, and I was irked because everyone seemed to expect a good time whereas last year no one had wanted to go, and I had gone through weeks of unending embarrassment. First, I had had to coax and plead to make them come; second, I had had to keep them in line when they did come; and third, I had had to argue the merits of the party afterward—which they insisted was horrible. Everyone *thought* I had been invited to the current affair; none of them could be argued out of the idea it would be really tremendous.

Robert seemed the person closest to me in the whole situation.

"So you're invited—but are you going to go?" I asked.

"I guess I will. All your friends are. Can you think of something better to do?"

The bell rang, and I accompanied him to his locker. "I thought you were my friend. You don't really want to, so why go?"

"Why not?" He took out a few books and started up the stairs. I had about given up. "Unless you feel like crashing the party, then I'll come with you like I was never invited."

I thought it over, but couldn't feel any enthusiasm for the

idea, and by the time school was over it had slipped my mind. But on the way home I ran into two friends who hadn't been invited either and were piqued like I was, and when I mentioned it casually, they thought immediately that it was a tremendous idea. If we crashed, we would—as Robert put it later—be pounding them to the dust with our presence; we would prove we were as good as they were, we would strike out at the hidden laughter, and as we walked along, I suddenly made the decision.

3

It seemed to me I spent a lot of time with Robert after that to insure his conversion to the side of the uninvited. Saturday night of the first week of November, a few hours before the party began, we waited in the kitchen for his mother to come home and tried to figure out exactly what we were going to do. He sat at the kitchen table leaning his head on his hand and not taking seriously anything I said.

"But I think," I insisted, "that she'll let us in because we know everybody there, and I used to be a wheel in the house. Don't you think so?"

He shrugged. He wore a dark suede jacket—even in the house—dress shirt and khakis. I had on pretty much the same. The party was formal.

"Oh, she will," I said. "She couldn't see us actually standing there on the doorstep and not let us in—could she?

"Yes."

"Stop being funny."

Then the back door opened, and Robert's stepmother came in with a large sack of groceries, followed by a little boy of four or five carrying a smaller bag. He had flaming red hair, a tremendous lot of freckles, and when he caught sight of me, his eyes bugged out. With great gentleness he set the bag on the sideboard, then glanced at me again. "Eggs," he said.

His mother smiled down at him. "Thank you very much, Paul. Now run along. It's time for your bath." When he had trotted off—rather reluctantly—she turned the smile on me.

"I suppose you're Jack. You're staying for dinner, aren't you?"

"I asked this morning, Ma," Robert said. "You said it would be all right."

She frowned. "I wish you wouldn't call me Ma. What do you call your mother, Jack?"

I swallowed hard, feeling uncomfortable. "I don't know. Sometimes I say Ma. I guess she doesn't like it either."

She brooded over this for a moment, then nodded. She was still in her twenties, I guessed, and it was hard to believe she was a real mother at all, not just some kind of older sister. She was tall and thin and had a sort of beaked nose like a hawk, but really she wasn't bad looking. Her hair was honey brown and long on her shoulders. Everything she did was brisk. She took off her coat, hung it on a hanger behind the door, washed her hands at the kitchen sink and began tying on a flowered plastic apron.

"I understand you're a sophomore at St. Francis, Jack. Do you live around here?"

"I used to," I said.

"Oh. Where?"

"On Ridgepoint."

"North or south?"

"North."

"Huh." She was unpacking the large grocery bag now, laying the items in a neat row: lettuce, tomatoes, a small pastry box, and four TV dinners. "You know, there are three sections to this town: one south of Wilshire, one north between Wilshire and Sunset, and one above Sunset. If our house was located above Wilshire, it would be worth a great deal more than it is. Did you ever know that?"

"I never thought about it much."

"Because you lived on the right side of Wilshire, that is why. I'll tell you something else. You can guess what section people live in by their cars. North Wilshire people drive bright Cadillacs and Sunset people drive Lincolns and black Cadillacs. Sometimes both kinds make me sick. Down here, below Wilshire——" She broke off, glanced at me sharply. "Ridgepoint . . . Are you Jack *Clark*?"

"Yes, ma'am," I admitted, feeling suddenly weak as if I had been pointed out in a line-up.

"Then you're the boy who was with Robert when he wrecked my car a few months ago! What on earth made the two of you do such a thing? And you're a year older, too. Do you know the repair bill was nearly three hundred dollars?"

"Ma—Mother," Robert interposed. "I told you a dozen times, it was my fault. Besides, the insurance company paid the bill."

"Yes," she said. "They also immediately canceled my policy—and your father's, too. He was furious. He had the same company for six years—never one accident. All they would say is that they don't carry policies with families that have teen-age drivers."

"I'm sorry," I said. And I felt sorry. Right then, I was convinced that the entire incident had been my fault, almost.

"Robert is sorry, too, I guess. He can't get a driver's license now when he's sixteen. He has to wait until he's eighteen."

The noise I was vaguely conscious of turned out to be Robert's fingers drumming on the table top; his voice was strained. "Thanks to you. You managed that. You told the cops I was unpredictable—that you wouldn't take any responsibility . . ."

"I was upset," she said. "Well, how would you feel? Coming home, our brand-new car gone, then a policeman at the door . . . 'We've got your son at City Hall, ma'am.' "

"Look, Mother," he stood up, "you don't have to fix dinner for us. We're kind of in a hurry."

"And where are you in such a hurry to?"

"A party."

"At five in the afternoon?"

"No. We're going visiting first." It was news to me.

"Who are you visiting?"

"I don't know. Thousands of people."

"Well, you can do your visiting after dinner. You asked if you could invite a friend, and I've made all the preparations."

He scowled at the four aluminum-wrapped trays on the sideboard. "Yes, you must need a rest after slaving all afternoon over a hot stove."

She stared at him, and the brisk coldness seemed to melt from her face so that she looked younger than ever, almost defenseless, but she turned away quickly before I could be sure that her eyes were wet.

"I don't pretend to be a fabulous cook, but I'm sure that I always serve nourishing meals, Robert," she said, her back turned. "You don't look exactly anemic—does he, Jack?"

"No, ma'am," I murmured.

"And it isn't much fun to come home and cook after working all day in an office, is it? Or wouldn't you know about that, Robert?" she asked, whirling around.

"You don't work Saturdays," Robert said, but his cheeks were flushed with embarrassment.

"No," she admitted. "I took Paul to the Zoo. I see so little of him during the week. Do you mind?"

"You don't have to work at all. My father said so. You just do it because you want to . . ."

She studied him for a moment and her face was cold again, her eyes hard. "It costs more to run a household and dress and feed two boys than your father realizes. Anyway, that's *my* business, isn't it? Isn't it my business?"

Robert looked miserable. "I'm sorry," he said. "All right?"

"Oh, sure, it's all right."

She popped the TV trays into the oven. "Now, if you can stop being in such a rush, you might set the table and then go check up on Paul."

I sat there feeling very much in the way, while Robert rattled around the dining alcove with silverware and glasses, then clumped off to check on Paul. After a moment, she looked over at me.

"Your mother doesn't work, I suppose, Jack? I mean, in an office or anywhere?"

"No, ma'am."

"What does your father do?"

"He's a lawyer with William, McCann, and Clark."

"If Mr. Garrety had an office in town, perhaps I—but he's away so much. Sometimes two or three weeks at a stretch. He travels, you know. This party tonight, where is it?"

"Brentwood."

"Who's giving it?"

"A girl. Kathy."

"Kathy who?" she insisted.

I didn't know why, but I felt trapped and ridden under. "Kathy Sheean."

Apparently she sensed my feeling, because she sighed and her thin cheeks crimsoned slightly. "Robert always thinks I'm prying, too, but I'm only trying to do my . . . duty. A mother should know her son's friends—and where both of them are going."

"I told you we were going to a party. Didn't you believe me?" said Robert rather loudly. I hadn't heard him come back, and she looked at him quickly and then away, a little guiltily.

"If this party is in Brentwood, shouldn't you wear different clothes?" she asked. "Slacks, a jacket?"

"It's . . . informal," he said. "By the way, Paul didn't drown. He couldn't find his sailboat, so I did, and now he's in an ocean."

"That was nice. You boys can go in the living room and watch television for a while, if you like. I'll call you when dinner's ready."

The living room was small and somewhat overcrowded with six- or seven-year-old furniture, which included two sofas, one hard to the feel and the other more luxurious. Everything was very neat. Robert switched the dial around, and we watched part of a newscast and then a children's program, which was laughable. After a few minutes, he began flipping through the pages of a magazine, and my thoughts returned to the party.

Only three hours now before it started. Would Kathy let us in? I tried to imagine us striding through the door, Kathy too shocked, too sorry to protest, me making sarcastic remarks, breaking her heart. How would I like to break her heart and have everyone know it? And then would I care? Would I ever care?

"Mother says dinner is ready." Paul was standing in the doorway, very little in a plaid flannel robe, his red hair still wet but neatly combed.

"How about a ride?" Robert said. Bending over, he let Paul climb onto his shoulders and carried him in solemn silence to the dinner table. Mrs. Garrety smiled, but there was a hint of annoyance in her eyes.

"He's getting too big for that."

"He's not that big," Robert told her. The exuberance left his face, though; he looked tired, almost sullen and began eating quickly. Besides the TV platters—thin slices of steaming beef, pale peas, and mashed potatoes—there were salad and hot rolls. He had finished before I was half through and his stepmother scarcely started.

"Did I tell you that your father phoned last night?" she asked.

"No," he said.

"He'll be home tomorrow. He sent you his love and asked how you were behaving."

"What did you say?"

"I said you were behaving all right, as far as I knew. So—keep it up if you want to take that trip."

He looked at her intently, his eyes very bright, searching, then he shrugged. "Thanks. Mind if we leave now?"

"There's dessert—French pastry."

"I'll eat it later. Do you want some French pastry, Jack?"

"I—I don't think I could eat it," I said. As a matter of fact, I was still hungry, but there was a strange sort of tension in that little alcove that made me uneasy, even though I couldn't understand it, and I was extremely happy with the idea of leaving.

She nodded and began to cut Paul's meat into smaller pieces, coaxing him to eat. "Paul and I will do the dishes, won't we, dear?"

"Yes, Mommy."

She brushed her fingers lightly over his red hair, then looked at me. "You know, Paul is exactly like his father—same husky build, too. All except for his eyes. Brown, like mine. Mr. Garrety has blue eyes."

Somehow I couldn't resist glancing from the small, freckled face to Robert, where he stood near the door, so utterly tall and different—brown-haired, cat-eyed, skin clear of marks. He returned my look and grinned.

"Mother, you'd better watch out. One day we'll be taking Paul with us to all of our little parties. Hey, Red, how would you like that?"

"Birthday parties?"

"With cake and ice cream and of course champagne. You must have champagne, Little Red."

"Robert, don't talk to the boy like that! And don't call him Red either!"

"Why not? Why can't I call him anything I want if he's my brother?"

She did not answer, but her eyes shone and somehow she reminded me of some wild bird guarding her young.

"Well," Robert repeated, "aren't you my brother, Paul?"

Terror filled the round brown eyes. Paul's mouth opened and his expression seemed to say, "Do not argue," but he kept silent.

She had found words at last. "I'll never understand you, Robert! Never, never. And Heaven knows it isn't because I haven't tried. Run along now, the both of you. Glad you came, Jack. Come again soon. Do."

"Thank you, Mrs. Garrety," I said. "It was a very fine dinner. I enjoyed it very much."

"So did I, Mother."

"Good." She nodded at me, stared at Robert, then looked down almost sadly at her own plate. "Wish *I* could—now." We were almost at the door. "What time will you be home?"

"I don't know—midnight."

"No later, please. Remember, your father comes in tomorrow."

The back door opened onto a small area that connected with the garage; the early evening air was crisp and fresh, and some clumps of chrysanthemums lined the driveway. We walked past them to the sidewalk. Robert seemed a little shaken, and neither of us said anything until we were halfway down the block. "How did you like the daily riot?" he asked.

I shrugged. "What's all this business about a trip?"

"Oh . . . there's some place I want to go and they keep promising to send me—if I'm good. 'You can go if you're good,' they say. 'Oh, you twisted the cat's tail; now you must stay home. Shame, Robert!' . . . Listen, do you want to know where we're going now?"

"Yes. It's much too early for the party."

"Well, I don't *know* where we're going," he said.

"What about Eric's house?" I thought we could play a little football.

"No!" He crossed the street which formed the intersection. "I just got a better idea. This girl, I followed her home once. She goes to L. A. High. Her name's Danni. We can beat her until it's time to go to the party."

There was still a good hour of sunlight remaining when we reached Danni's house. It had been a hot day, and it was still a warm, cool-shadowed late afternoon, and there weren't any clouds in the sky; there wasn't any breeze. I was being initiated to the wandering travels we were to repeat on afternoons and weekends later on, dropping in on people, picking up girls. When we said we were going out, we never knew exactly where. Danni lived below Wilshire, like Robert, but even below Wilshire there was a social difference, because Westside, though no one ever spoke of it as the West Side, was upper class, and Eastside, where Robert lived, was middle class. There were a lot of upper class apartment buildings on the West Side, and two-story private houses, but it was all within a few blocks of the business section. The façade of Danni's house was shingled and painted spanking white, and there was a small, neat front yard. The door had a brass knocker and a lace-curtained wicket.

Danni opened the door. She was a little girl, plump, with short brown hair. She had a faintly pretty Jewish face, and she wore a tight wool skirt and a breast-swollen blouse.

"Danni, hi!" Garrety said, walking inside. "You remember me. Vince—the handsome one."

She looked at us a little puzzled. "Oh yes. I guess!"

"I talked to you on the bus!"

She nodded. "Well, won't you– I guess you're already in!"

"Yes," he said, "I guess we are."

"Would–would you like some cokes, or something?"

"Cokes? Please–it's so adult."

"Well, sit down," she said, and started out for the kitchen.

"Anybody else home?" Robert asked.

She shook her head.

"Isn't she hideous?" he whispered to me. He gave to each word a nasal half drawl, which I was beginning to use on crushing occasions too.

"I think she's about to throw us out," I responded. "Why can't you be more polite?"

"Oh, please, she loves me! Couldn't you tell? I'm going in the kitchen to beat her." He took hold of my arm and pointed to a counter bar and a row of glass cabinets. "There's the bar. Get a bottle for us, they've got thousands. And be prepared to take her over, so I can roam through the house." He headed for the kitchen.

I went into the living room, but found the bar locked. I took stock of the room: three or four coffee tables were distributed in front of as many couches, and each table bore more than one cigarette lighter. The whole place was overfurnished. I began to feel frisky, all alone in the room and more or less in command. I visited the den, returned to the living room, and then moved into the pantry. The house was overflowing with cigarette lighters. Pushing open the door to the kitchen, I saw Robert with his arms around Danni's waist as she poured soft drinks into glasses.

"How did you succeed?" he asked.

I shook my head.

"What do you mean, succeed?" Danni asked.

He dropped his hands from her waist. "Oh, he's looking for the men's room. He's too embarrassed to ask." He started out of the kitchen. "I left something in the living room. Don't worry about me!"

The girl and I were alone together. "What did he leave?" She was piqued and a little suspicious, and her lipstick was smeared.

"I don't know. I think he lost a dollar bill."

"Is that all?" She put her hands on her hips and scowled. "What about those cokes?"

I shrugged. "We'll still drink them."

"What about his?"

"I don't know: let's bring one out to him!"

"He can just get it himself! *What's he doing in the living room?*"

"Well, I guess he's hunting for the dollar," I said.

She was halfway out the door before I had finished. I caught up with her in the pantry and threw my arm around her shoulders; she let it stay there as she pushed open the door.

We saw Robert behind the bar, stacking empty bottles up on the counter. He stared at us. "I was just getting them out of the way."

Danni stalked behind the bar, put her hands on her hips, and looked him in the eye.

"Do you want your coke or don't you?"

"Oh yes, Danni—please get it for me."

"All right," she said. "Now sit down and don't move till I come back!"

"Beat the upstairs," Robert whispered, as she hurried out. "Pound the carpet, so she'll run up after you."

I ran up the stairs, peeked into two or three bedrooms, and began heavily pacing back and forth along the hallway.

"Why didn't your friend use the powder room down here?" I heard Danni say. "And why's he making all that racket?"

Garrety murmured something. I could hear her move to the foot of the stairs.

"Are you in trouble?" she called.

I opened and closed a few doors and waited.

"Come down here!"

I dog-trotted the length of the hallway and back. She ran up the stairs. I ducked into what I judged was her bedroom (let her find me) and picked up a small photograph on the dresser. It showed a pretty girl with an angry, aggressive glance. "Who's this, Danni?"

She came over to identify it. "My girl friend."

"She's pretty. Is she jealous of you, your girl friend?"

"Very funny."

"Girls *get* jealous."

"So do boys!"

I slipped my arms around her; as before she did not resist them. She turned to the left, and I kissed her left cheek, turned to the right, more petulantly, and I kissed her right cheek, she lifted her chin up, and I kissed her neck. Finally I made her lips, soft at first, but picking up in pressure.

There was thumping downstairs.

She sprang from my arms. "What's he up to?"

"I don't know," I said, "hunting for his dollar again, I guess."

"He's up to something!" she said and wheeled out of the room.

I reached her at the top of the stairs; she wavered, then

skipped away. I caught her again just before she reached the landing, kissed her, lost my balance, and falling backward pulled her on top of me. I was almost crushed. It had been months since I kissed a girl, or held one in my arms, and now I was being sat on by Danni.

"Let go of me," she said.

"All right—get off!" When she had shifted half her weight off my body, I kissed her again. "You're lovely."

"You're so hard up," she said angrily. She beat her fists against my chest, sprang to her feet, and hurried downstairs.

I followed her down as quickly as I could. Then I heard the back door slam mysteriously.

"What was that?" she asked. "Where is he?"

"I don't know."

"My parents will be back soon—you guys had better be gone."

The front door opened. I turned toward it anxiously. It was Garrety.

"What have you been doing?" Danni cried.

"Nothing. I was just wandering around and seeing what the house looked like."

Her eyes darted down to one of the coffee tables. "You haven't even finished your coke."

"Oh, who wants a hideous coke?" He put his arm around her. "Oh, Danni, you're so gorgeous. Turn on the TV. Bring us something to eat, and then we will make merry."

She wriggled her shoulders distastefully. "I'm not going to get you anything. I'm not going to let you out of my sight."

"Oh no, I'm too handsome."

"You're too conceited!"

She moved to the front door with Robert clinging to her.

"My mother and father will be *home* in a few minutes," she said.

"Of course, I believe you."

"I mean it," she cried. "Will you please go?"

"Oh, all right," Robert said. "Good-by."

She grunted and slammed the door behind us.

"What did you get?" I asked when we reached the sidewalk.

"Champagne. I found it in some pantry cabinet." He plucked it out of a row of hedges, and slipped it beneath his jacket where it bulged out as we walked along.

Before we were halfway down the block, a long, black Cadillac pulled in Danni's driveway.

"See? We got out just in time," I said.

"We'll have to go back some day. Isn't it hilarious?"

"Yes."

We went another block before he ducked in between some screening hedges in somebody's front yard, sat down on the ground, and pulled the cork out of the champagne bottle.

I drank a little and felt a shudder of nausea pass through me.

"What's the matter?"

"I hate it."

"Hell, it's good!"

I drank a little more and said, "Yeah, I guess so," and left the rest to him.

But he didn't drink very much.

"Should we save it for tonight?" I asked.

"No, then we'd have to be carrying it all around. Where shall we go now?"

I shrugged my shoulders.

"We could have gone to Julie's house, but now it's too late. Danni was more hilarious."

"Who's Julie?"

"Julie? She's this dame about sixteen. Her father's in the movies. He beats her. She's about three inches taller than I am."

I was interested. "If you're sure it's too late, then let's go up to the drive-in and talk to people," I said.

We abandoned the champagne and started back up the street. I criticized him for calling everything "hideous," and we decided finally to sometimes shorten the word to "hid," so it wouldn't lose its impact.

At the drive-in, I found I had run out of cigarettes, and reached into Robert's pocket for one. (I smoked, but hadn't learned how to inhale.) I brought out a few firecrackers and a smoke bomb.

"Where'd you get these?" I asked.

"I got them. They're for tonight—just in case. Or otherwise."

We drank coffee and talked to a few acquaintances who came in from time to time. Then, at seven-thirty, we met the other boys—Bill and Frank. Robert showed them the firecrackers, but none of us thought we'd have to use them. It would be foolish of Kathy, we argued, to leave us on the doorstep.

Well, we couldn't hitchhike a ride to Kathy's house, and it was getting close to nine o'clock and the party was an hour old. Bill suggested we take a taxi and split the bill. We did, but the fact of our being in a taxi with no way back made me more afraid and more embarrassed.

The cab left us off one house down from hers. Guest cars,

silent and formidable, were lined up a block long, and when we reached the entrance to her yard and saw the long circle driveway and the well-lighted, two-story house, with strings of bright lamps decorating the pillars flanking the front door, we felt less ambitious about crashing the place than ever.

4

You couldn't see or hear what was going on in the house from the outside. I was already conscious of my everyday clothes and began to realize how hard it would be to think up anything to say to Kathy that would assure us a welcome. We were a rather messy looking group, I thought.

"You ring the bell," Bill said.

"Why don't you, and I'll wave from the lawn, so she'll know I'm here," I answered.

"Oh, let's all just ram the door," Garrety said.

So we all ran up to the door. I knocked in triumph, turned my head and found they had melted someways in back of me. As I moved after them in a kind of panic, the door opened.

Kathy's grandmother stood there.

"Can we come in?" I murmured.

She was short and rather plump, with Spanish eyes and white hair done up high in ringlets; she wore a black dinner dress that added a regal note, but the smile she gave me, after one startled moment, was embarrassed. I saw that she thought I was still a nice boy and wished to welcome me in spite of everything, and this made me want to run.

"Good evening, Jack," she said. "I don't know . . . Wait here a moment, please." She disappeared, leaving the door slightly ajar.

We moved forward to the lintel, encouraged by her graciousness. We could see inside. The guests were seated at little tables on the patio; we could hear their dishes clanking and their polite, happy voices. They were somehow fearsome, formidable, unearthly. Somewhere among them, a small orchestra tuned up.

Then we saw the grandmother emerging again, and Kathy was with her. Kathy was very tall, her complexion was clear and tan, there was grace in her body; she wore a white organdy dress with an orchid pinned on her shoulder. She seemed majestic, faultless, and she made me a little afraid.

I forgot whatever magic words I had devised, and I asked hoarsely, "Can we come inside?"

"No," she said, reaching her hand out for the knob, "I'm afraid you can't."

The door closed suddenly. I was stunned. The dinner sounds and the murmur of the partygoers ended—we would never join them. A desperate enthusiasm took hold of me. "The die has been cast!"

Robert clapped me on the back. We were all laughing happily, greatly relieved that we had taken the rebuff and it had been no harder than it was.

We stole around the side of the house and peeked through the hedges at the guests. They were just finishing dinner apparently, and a few were getting up to dance to the orchestra, which had begun to play. The first one we recognized was

Mike MacKyntyre, a sophomore, who was chatting with a pretty blond girl seated at his table.

We were light-headed with envy and longing.

Robert leaned forward. "Who's the hideous child hating him secretly as he thinks he makes conquests?" He took out a firecracker. "Should I blow him up with it?"

We stuck it in the ground, touched a match to the fuse, then ran around to the front of the house. The powder ignited loudly and carried a sharp echo, and we fled jubilantly into the street. But there was no visible reaction at the house. We stole back into the yard. The orchestra was playing. We hadn't made a dent.

Robert produced another firecracker, which Bill lit and heaved quickly into some hedges.

We shouted, "Get out, Kathy!" after the detonation. There was no response, nothing. Suddenly we were panicked at the thought of ridicule and retribution, and had there been some other place to go that night, we would have gone—quickly.

Robert suggested more explosions and organized cheering, but we were no longer in the mood. I didn't notice when he slipped away. But suddenly he was racing up the front steps with a smoking object in hand. He crossed the porch, jerked open the wicket, screamed, and threw his burden inside. We retreated to the entrance of the driveway with wildly beating hearts.

"What did you set off, Garrety?" we asked as he rejoined us.

"A stink bomb!"

Smoke blossomed out the wicket. In the distance the orchestra died.

The door banged open, and we could see figures passing to and fro in a cloud that slowly drifted outside. Two figures actually stepped out from the door. They turned out to be freshmen—friends of Robert.

"What a riot," one of them panted.

"What happened?" we asked, overwhelmed with success.

"We've been bombed! Nobody knows what to do—the party's gone haywire—the girls are in tears."

"The girls are in tears?" I repeated.

"Look!" It was like a delegation, a peace parlay. Her grandmother was first in the procession, then came her mother, and after her, two boys, who looked uncertain. Her grandmother came halfway around the driveway before halting and clasping her hands together.

"What is it you boys are after?"

We laughed.

"Oh, Granny," Garrety called out, "get us some whisky, and we won't beat you!"

"What?"

"Bring us some scotch on the rocks, please—not too much seltzer in mine, and then get out."

"What's the matter with you boys?" she cried.

"Nothing," Bill said. "We're having a party of our own!"

She retreated in bewilderment. In exhilaration at our revenge, I slugged Robert's shoulder. He had stood up for me, saved my face, and caused the girls to cry.

The door closed on the little group, but a minute later it opened again, letting out a police squad of a dozen or so older guys who advanced nonchalantly, making fists of their hands.

"Let's get out of here," someone whispered.

We turned and ran, six of us, up the dark, residential block, then down a side street. We kept laughing in our fear, and none of us looked back. We spotted a garage which was separated from a darkened house, and moved behind it. We sat down against a wall, all in a row, and laughed and spoke in whispers. Our hands were trembling.

"Anybody after us?" we kept asking each other. "Shh! . . . Shh!" "Anybody got a cigarette?" "Don't light up yet. Listen." "God—an army charges after us."

"How was the party?" Bill asked our pair of recruits.

"Are you kidding?" the taller one said. "By the way, Robert, Kathy's sister said, 'Oh guy, that couldn't be Robert Garrety out there, could it?' "

"So what did you say?" Robert asked.

"I said, 'Well, I *really* couldn't tell you, dear.' "

"Good, then I can still beat her, and she'll say, 'Oh, Robert, won't you come to all my parties?' But tell me, who else did you see? Did you see a girl named Ann Fields there?"

"I don't know. What does she look like?"

"Oh, she's blond and kind of casual, and she has these real blue eyes!"

"I don't know."

"Why do you beat everybody, Garrety?" I asked after a short silence.

"Yeah, Garrety?" Bill demanded.

"I don't beat *you*." That seemed to clear things up, but he went on a little desperately: "I could've gone tonight, but I didn't want to because they serve tea afterwards, and I'm *sorry*, but that is hideous and a thousand rules of etiquette required and the grandmother—you look up, and you see a wrinkle—and the opera playing." He looked off. "Hey, don't I hear something?"

"I don't think so," I said.

Again it turned out to be nothing, and we began to figure we hadn't been followed after all. We decided to make our way out.

"They can recognize Jack and me," Robert broke in, "so you guys go on ahead. We'll follow in five minutes when the coast is clear."

They agreed and stole back into the street.

He borrowed one of my cigarettes. "Well, I hope my father isn't beaten with information when he returns."

"About tonight?"

He nodded. "Or else the trip will be off."

We kept silent for a few minutes. I kept feeling he wanted to tell me something. It grew time to follow the others, but still we sat there. I cleared my throat. He sighed.

"Guess where I'm going—never," he said.

"Where?"

"New York."

"Why?"

"True Ma."

"Oh. How long will you be there?"

"A week or two— I don't know."

"And it is up to your father to send you?"

He sighed and leaned back. "Yes, so I can meet untrue father and baby sis and see Ma again."

"Well—then why'd you come with me tonight?"

"Why not? Anything to beat people."

"Don't you really want to see your mother?"

"Yes."

"Good. I hope you go."

Suddenly he was shaking my hand. "Congratulations. You're the only one outside of me."

"How can *I* be the only one?"

He shrugged. "Just believe it." He put out his cigarette. "I'll tell you really why I want to go."

"Why?"

He glanced at me hesitantly, then leaned his back against the wall and looked away. "Oh, make a guess first."

"I don't know," I said. "Because sons like to visit their mothers once in a while."

"No."

"Then why?"

"You taken a look at me?"

I nodded.

"You taken a look at my father?"

"I saw his picture."

"*I'm sure.*"

It didn't get through to me right away. "What does that mean?"

His eyes shone, and he was sullen, contemplative, and the fact that I didn't understand suddenly made it unpleasant and painful to him. "Do you want me to draw a map for you? You saw Paul, the little replica of the father? You saw him, didn't you? Well, do we look alike?"

I was stunned and *wouldn't* believe. "*You're nuts!*"

He shook his head. "Listen, I've known this a long time. I've got a true mother and a false mother, a true father and a false father, but I think my true father isn't my true father even. He's a false true-father!"

"But you don't *know*."

"My mother will tell me. I can't write it in a letter, and I can't ask *him*. He doesn't even like to talk about my mother, and if I said something like that he'd throw me out of the house. Maybe he doesn't even know himself."

"What makes you think it's true?"

"A lot of things—the face mostly; but there are other things, too. Hints."

He sounded too stubborn to argue with; I didn't know whether I wanted to argue, but I certainly didn't want to agree when I knew so little about his circumstances.

"Have you ever talked to anyone like this before?"

"No."

"Well, c'mon." His not having told anybody else seemed to make it more my concern.

We got up and without another word went out on the street and headed back for Sunset.

He cuffed my shoulder. "You won't tell anyone, will you, Jack?"

"No." We turned the corner and we could see the party breaking up much too early down the block.

"Jack! We're buddies—right?"

"Right!" We shook hands. It was dramatic. It had taken two years of preliminaries but finally, in one sad night, we were friends, and our separate torments now belonged to both of us.

She *was* crying in that quieting house, I knew it, I knew it even then.

5

Anyway, I sent her a card at Christmas time, mysteriously signed 'J'. Weeks later a repercussion of our raid had hit my mother. Kathy wasn't going to have any more parties *at all,* and I had something to do with it. I received no punishment because everyone was so vague about what I had 'done'—including her parents and particularly her father, who had been out of town.

She didn't send me a Christmas card; I scarcely expected her to. I spent a lot of my time wondering what I could do to make her forget the vandalization of her pride and if she would ever forgive me.

But Robert was happy. As the holiday drew closer, he became more and more certain that a plane ticket to New York would be his Christmas present.

On the day before Christmas I went over to his house, so that we could pick up a few last minute gifts at a near-by jewelry store. It was a warm afternoon, and there was a milky sky with the tops of buildings and trees standing out neatly against it, dark-edged. Most of the trees were bare, trunks and branches mottled gray, and there was a slight northerly breeze that picked up dust, papers, and leaves and slid them neatly to one side of the lawns. The breeze crackled the dead fronds of the banana tree in Robert's yard and stirred a bush that was bright with Hibiscus.

His father opened the door. It was like seeing small Paul as a full-grown man. Mr. Garrety had dark red hair, a freckled complexion, and luminous blue eyes. He was tall and robust with a hearty grin. He was ten or twelve years older than his wife, still a young man, and a man who would probably look no older in ten or twelve more years.

"Oh," he said with his grin, "you must be for Robert. Well, come in. I'm his father."

The small living room was overcrowded with a sparsely branched silver tip that reached within an inch or two of the ceiling. It was clogged with silver tinsel through which shone colored lights, and hung with blue, silver, and red Christmas bulbs. It was very merry and bright, but Robert, sitting slumped in a leather chair, stared at it fiercely. He glanced at me without changing expression, then turned back to the tree.

Mrs. Garrety nodded at me from a small sofa near the window, invited me to sit down. But there was tension in the air, and I had uneasy misgivings.

"Thank you," I said. "I can't stay. Where is that jewelry store, Robert?"

He looked at me again, then got slowly to his feet. "Corner of Woodglen and Santa Monica. What took you so long?"

"It isn't late," I said. "Can we leave now?"

"May I go with Jack now?" Robert asked.

"Not just yet," his father said. "I don't think we've ended our discussion."

"What more is there to discuss?"

"Your attitude." Mr. Garrety lit a cigarette, started to put the pack away, then turned to me apologetically. "I'm sorry. Do you smoke?"

"No, thanks."

He was in a hostly mood. "Perhaps we can get you some Christmas eggnog."

"No, thanks."

He smiled speculatively. "Ever had any?"

"Oh no, sir."

"Oh, never!" Robert said.

I forced down the corners of my mouth. Robert's levity didn't decrease the tension in the least, and I felt that far from helping his case, my presence was only making him more reckless.

There were little approaching footsteps and then Paul, freshly bathed, appeared and stopped dead still when he saw me. His mother asked if he remembered me, and he finally did, and then no longer afraid, he went past me and up to his father and asked him to guess what he had done today.

"Did you see Santa Claus? . . . Then I can't guess."

"I gave my teacher a Christmas card."

I looked at the father and son, heads together as they pondered this, and I knew Robert had a very good point to raise about his paternity. His father's hair was a darker red than Paul's, and he didn't have nearly as many freckles, and his eyes were blue not brown, but the resemblance was overwhelming.

"I'm talking to your big brother now," Mr. Garrety finally said. "Why don't you go out and play?"

"He's just taken a bath," his mother protested.

"Then go play soldiers in your room." It took five minutes of persuasion, but Paul went.

"Christmas," Mr. Garrety said. "Harmony . . . Carols . . . Gifts . . . You boys will be older soon—five, ten years from now, you'll realize Christmas can mean absolutely nothing . . . unless *you* put something into it. A man's whole life could be measured by the number of his happy Christmases."

It was embarrassing to listen to this speech, but there was an anxiety mixed in, too, because the speech was not being delivered for its own sake.

"When we're very young," he went on, "we seldom think about making others happy. But when we're grown up, generosity is no longer a matter of free will—it's your duty, and it's with you every hour of the day. You can shirk it, but you'll never feel right about it. And Christmas—at least it's always seemed that way to me—is just the essence of that duty to provide happiness."

We were intensely silent. I breathed cautiously in measured breaths, as if to be normal was also to be careless and invite ruin.

"Awfully hard." He smiled, and I suddenly became aware he was smiling at me. "If *you* wanted to go away over Christmas, Jack—just suppose—and your family couldn't afford to send you, would you understand their viewpoint, or would you go around muttering that they hated you?"

"I didn't," Robert shouted.

"Yes, you did. Your mother heard you."

"Then she's a liar!"

"I heard you!" He was obviously trying to control his anger.

"You've missed the whole point. You seem to have added stupidity to your other faults!"

Robert sprang to his feet, stalked into the hallway, and the whole house quivered with the slam of his bedroom door.

Mrs. Garrety stirred on the sofa. "We told him he could go a month from now, during the semester holidays." Her glance flickered to Mr. Garrety.

He was staring into the deserted hallway, the freshly lit cigarette in his mouth, and I suddenly thought how terrible it must be to be obliged to see others happy. "I'm sorry," I said to him. "He should just have made up his mind to go in January, I guess." I looked down at the floor. "I have to be going." I got up. "Well, Merry Christmas!"

"Merry Christmas!" they echoed. I went out.

We got up early Christmas morning because of my brother, who was eleven. After we had opened the presents, my father went back to sleep; we roused him for breakfast, and after eating started to dress for church.

When the doorbell rang, I was the only one ready and ran downstairs to answer it.

Robert was standing on the steps. I was so surprised, I couldn't say anything for a minute. His face was red, but his eyes shone.

"Morning," I said. "How do you come to be here?"

"Oh, I was just passing by." He happened to live three miles away. "Are you going to let me in?"

I let him in, and he sat down on an armchair in front of the Christmas tree. "What's going on?" I asked.

He shrugged. "I been kicked out."

"On Christmas?"

"Why not?"

"Why don't you tell me about it?"

"Why don't you forget about it?"

I strode around the Christmas tree, readjusting shivers of tinsel. "You might as well tell me."

He lit a cigarette. "I thought walking would cool me off, but I just feel lousier."

"Tell me then."

He unbuttoned his jacket. "Yesterday we were going to the jewelry shop, remember? Well, there was a thousand hints by supposedly true father, and I really made it two inches out the front door."

I nodded.

"After you left I had to stay in my bedroom—no dinner and truces and a hundred conferences, and untrue mother screaming, 'Oh, I don't want any discord in this house.' So finally the axe was buried. But by then it was too late."

"Too late?"

"All the stores were closed. I couldn't buy my brother's present. So I did the next best thing, of course."

"Yeah?"

"I put the six dollars in the card and I wrote, 'Dear Broth', buy yourself a Mickey Mouse watch with this.' So this morning my brother opened the card and showed it around and there was tremendous silence from the untrue people. I said, 'What's the matter?' True father, he got up and he collared me and he said, 'God damn, God damn,' and I said, 'Watch it,' and true father he went, 'Uh!' and he slammed me against the wall."

"He did?"

"Yeah. And Paul, my brother, was watching bug-eyed, and

my mother was screaming, 'Oh,' and my father just stood there, rather angry you could tell, his hands all shaking, and everybody was hating me. So I opened the door, and nobody seemed to object, and the tears, the hideous tears were about to come, so I said, 'God damn yourself—how hideous you all are,' and then I split."

He smiled.

"Why do you think your father got angry?"

"Slighting true son—the little one who is real."

I shrugged. "Well, my heart is broken. Do you want to wait around here?"

"No, if I'm gone long, untrue father will throw a spasm."

"Take it easy," I said.

"You'll have to tell me some hideous secrets about you sometime."

He went out. As I passed the living room window, I caught a glimpse of him disappearing down the sidewalk. I wished there was something I could do. But there wasn't anything; there never was.

6

My parents went into a marital crisis after New Year's, and before it was resolved, I came home almost every day to violently slammed doors, cold dinners or no dinners, solitary drives 'around the block' that lasted half the night, orders to pack my bags and come along with my mother, orders to unpack my bags and stay with my father. My parents were too upset with each other to be really upset about my poor semester report, though I was warned it should not happen again.

And though I was protected by living in a world my parents did not know, still sometimes at night before I fell asleep I worried over what it would be like to have a false mother and a false father like Robert, having to live with only one of my parents, my brother with me or not with me, the old order gone, having to choose between my parents, deciding, perhaps, which I should not love.

I worked up a brood about Kathy and how terribly I had hurt her—sweet and majestic as she had looked that night, and every night, and in every place I had ever seen her. I cursed myself continually for having been thrown out of her social orbit, the combination rich-and-young-gentlemen set, through mistaking the father of a hostess for a butler and demanding he bring me a drink. Having moved from the old neighborhood, I was out of contact with Kathy's society, even the casual fringe of it. With all that, and even though she was richer than I was, I didn't think it would be absolutely impossible to turn everything aright.

Robert's father got in touch with "true mother" and reported that she was too busy to receive her son during the January holidays.

"I knew it, I knew it, I knew it," Robert said. "Who goes visiting in January anyway?"

On the evening of the semester holiday, he came over to my house for dinner and ended up staying the night. Having made the decision to do so near ten o'clock, neither my parents nor Robert's father could do much about it, though they didn't like it. My parents associated him with my downward scholastic way, and his father always seemed peeved about whatever he did. However, from the way they spoke over the phone, I suspected something more substantial was behind his father's attitude now.

"What is it this time?" I asked when we were alone in my room.

He sat down with a bunch of comic books he had stolen from my brother, opened the first page of *The Batman,* then closed the cover and threw it on the floor. "I don't know." He picked up a horror comic and stretched out on the army cot we had unpacked for him. There was a short silence. He turned to page two. "Maybe it's because I took a shot at him."

I started. "You what!"

His shoulders twitched. "Just what I told you. Now go to hell with your prying, will you?"

I was exasperated; I thought, he had invited himself, too. "You stupid moron, back to Kindergarten!"

"Stupid moron yourself."

"Go to hell." I switched off the lights and jumped in bed.

He sprang up from the cot, switched them on again. "Wise up, I'm trying to read!"

"Talk lower, moron."

"I'll think about it!"

"Son-of-a-bitch," I said, more as a substitute for taking the Lord's name than as a descriptive noun. But s.o.b. was the worst thing I could have said.

He changed colors, leapt on my bed frantically. I kicked him back, got to my feet, and lowered my head into his stomach. He crashed to the floor, and I landed on top of him. For a few seconds I worried that I might have hurt him, but when he toppled me I knew I was in for it. He righted himself, jumped on me, and pinned my shoulders to the floor. "*Give?*"

I didn't answer, but I was relieved; I had begun to suspect he was a maniac. I exerted all my strength to the right side, trying to topple him, but didn't succeed. I waited five seconds, toppled him the second time, and sprang to my feet. After a minute of wrestling, I got a headlock on him and squeezed his neck until he was bent double over the floor. When I saw he was still game, I let go.

"All right—that's enough."

His face was flaming red, his hair stuck up wildly. "Goddamn you!"

I had fought out my resentment. "Take it easy."

"Shut up!"

"I didn't mean anything personal by what I said."

"If I thought you did, I'd still be fighting you."

"Okay," I said. "Just a minute." I looked out in the hallway to see if my parents had awakened, but heard nothing.

When I turned back, he was sitting on the edge of the cot. The second comic book was now face down on the floor. "They didn't wake up, did they?"

"No." I began pacing up and down. I knew now I wouldn't be able to go to sleep for some time.

He stared at the wall. "Maybe I should tell you what happened."

I shrugged. "Do you hate your father?"

"No."

"Why did you shoot at him?"

"I don't know. I didn't really shoot at him. He thinks I did, that's all."

"What did he do?"

Robert shrugged. "He took my .22 away and he said, 'I'm going to break it,' but he didn't. He hid it. Hah!"

"What did you shoot at?"

"I shot at the ceiling above the door."

"Where was he at the time?"

"At the time he was standing in the door."

"What was the argument about?"

He lit a cigarette. "I don't know—he was chopping the memory of true mother. So I chopped untrue mother, and untrue mother, well—steppy—tried to make it seem like I was jealous of little brother."

"So?"

"So I beat my room for hours, and I was cleaning my .22

when my father opened the door. He was scowling so I merely shot the ceiling, and he said, 'My God, my God, what kind of a son do I have?' and steppy ran around crying, 'Oh, we have to end this, we have to end this,' and then I said I was sorry and that you were expecting me."

"Why did you shoot the ceiling?" I asked.

"I don't know. I thought it would cause a little excitement." He put out the cigarette. "I'm not out to get my father. I don't feel that way. I don't care what he does, really."

I thought a minute. "Well, are we at peace?"

"I guess so. Shake!"

We shook hands. I turned off the lights and got under the sheets. Across the room I could just see the back of his head propped up on a pillow.

"Jack, you know why I hit you, don't you?" he asked.

"No." I closed my eyes and turned over.

"Because you insulted my mother. I didn't want you to think it was because you turned the lights off. Hell." He paused. "I wonder why my mother doesn't want to see me. Do you wonder?"

"She's busy." I shrugged.

"She's an actress, did I ever tell you that?"

"Yes."

"She's running around playing different people, and money is paid. And stardom is wished for. Once she wrote me to watch her on television. She was on twenty seconds. She blew her line."

I turned crimson. "What the hell."

"I know she's done better things. The last time I saw her in person was three years ago. I mean, she was playing in a road show in L.A. She came up to the house; the last two times I saw her she was stewed."

My eyes opened. Again he was telling me things I was sure he had never told anybody else. "What was she like?"

"I don't know. She was always saying, 'Robert, you're just full of mischief.' But she'd encourage me. She filled me with candy. It would be rather hectic living with her. She's very pretty—even steppy will tell you—and she doesn't look as old as she really is."

"How old?"

"Thirty-five, maybe. I don't know exactly how old she is. But she ain't a bag. I'm going to see her this summer—that's what they tell me *now*, anyway. Ha, ha." He paused. "I'm writing her a letter. I've torn it up five times, no lie. Now and then she writes long letters to me, and I haven't answered in months."

"Why don't I write it for you?"

"Would you? Thanks!"

An idea came to me suddenly as though out of a dream. "But wait a minute. I'll do it only if you write a letter for me in exchange."

"To who?"

I had to tell him all about it. I was past sleeping now. I got out of bed and turned on the light. "Kathy."

"Why?" he laughed.

"Can you keep a secret? I'm sorry for what we did. God, I've been sorry a long time. Really."

"Oh. You never mentioned it. What do you want me to say in the letter?"

"I don't know. Get up."

"Are we going to write it now?"

"Now."

He got up and looked at me with strained tolerance. "Why do we have to write it now?"

"Why not? But let's go downstairs where we don't have to be so quiet."

We dressed and stole downstairs into the kitchen. He sat at the table with a pen and paper, and I began pacing up and down.

"'Dear Kathy,'" I said. "'I'm a friend of Jack Clark. I have been observing—'"

"How do you spell observing?"

"O-b-s-e-r-v-i-n-g. 'I have been observing him lately, and I believe he is quite remorseful.' No. 'Quite saddened.' No. Garrety, what am I?"

"Depressed."

"That's right. 'He is quite depressed.' How did you know, Garrety?"

He looked around. "Well—I am, too."

"You are?"

"Yes, a thousand depressions. This girl, I hate her. I am depressed all days because of her."

"Which girl?"

"You wouldn't know her."

"What's her name?"

"Ann Fields, she lives in Westwood."

"I know her."

She was a blonde of my own age—pretty, buxom and athletic, with very striking blue eyes. He said he had danced with her one night at a party, got her phone number, and later in the week called up and talked to her for two solid hours. But he had been so overwhelmed, he had forgotten to tell her he had no car. So it didn't turn out; he never talked to her again, and she had a boy friend now. She was a mystery. A pretty girl is always older than a boy her same age, and he was a year-and-a-half younger than she to begin with. He had seen her here and there since October. Once he could have talked to her, but he didn't; he had been afraid.

I thought that was funny. "So that's why you asked about her that night we crashed Kathy's party? I think she's too old for you, that's what I think. Sorry."

"I think Kathy's too tall for you, if you want to know. Sorry!"

Now I was depressed. "I'm still growing. Don't worry about it."

"I'm not worried about it." He laughed and lit a cigarette. "Listen," he explained, "it makes no difference if Ann's older than I am. I beat all the older women. And—besides," he said, rocking his chair back, "you're older than I am, and you're my best friend."

"What do you want from people," I said, "substitute mothers and fathers?"

"No." He grimaced in distaste. "I've got four real ones already. It's just that I admire her. Slightly. I'm going to see her tomorrow night."

"Where?"

"In this Chi-ro Club in Westwood. I heard in school that she's mad at her boy friend, so I'm moving in."

"I used to belong to that club," I said. "You can't attend the meetings unless you're a member or a member brings you. Maybe Mike MacKyntyre can get us in . . . continue the letter." Something had been building in the back of my mind for a long time, and then I knew what it was. I was all locked up inside. I took down a square-shaped bottle from the cabinet and poured out some straight gin shots, holding my nose to avoid becoming nauseated.

He grinned. "Having a merry time, eh?"

"Stinking. I never did this before. How do people drink this stuff?"

"I think they mix it with something."

"Like——?"

He shrugged. "Like—I don't know—soft drinks, orange juice . . ."

I opened the refrigerator, found some orange juice, and then went over to the table and reread the one line of the letter.

"Sign it," I said.

He signed it in huge letters.

"'P.S.,'" I said. I began pouring out orange juice mixes and taking them fast, shuddered with each sip. "'My dear girl'"—my tongue said words I had never heard it say before—"'Jack has often spoken to me of you, and I think you are why he is depressed. I am writing this as a friend——'"

"You already said that."

"Keep writing: 'He thinks very highly of you, and he is very, very, very sorry.'"

"How many 'very's'?"

"Never mind."

"Is that the end of the letter?"

"Yes." I pushed him off the chair, sat down, and studied what he had written; when I finished, I crumpled it up in my hand.

He was laughing behind me.

I mixed another horrible orange-gin, but suddenly I choked, felt sicker, and didn't want any more. I took my head in my hands and thought about Kathy; I thought of her in her white dress, so sweet and forbidden that night; I saw the door being slammed in my face. I could see and feel that night again and what she had meant to me again, and I had a strange light feeling inside as if laughter and tears were mixed up and spinning out together, like colored flashes in a long dream, a whirlwind of joy and pain.

"Come on," Robert said, putting his hand on my shoulder. "C'mon, you better get up to bed."

"Get away."

"Look, Jack, why don't you just phone her right now and get it over with?"

"Shut up!"

"What if your parents find you here?"

I saw him throw the smoke bomb again, and run again, and I felt the same emotions, the intense desire not to have her cry but still to cry for me, because nobody had ever cried for me. "Shut up, bastard! You *bastard!*"

As I started to rise I saw his fist come at me, and I took such a long time to fall I remembered laughing a little; then, suddenly, I was sitting on the floor trying to figure how long I had been there; my mouth hurt, and the electric lights hurt my eyes.

"Jack! I'm sorry!" He started to lift me up. "Are you all right?"

I flailed out. "Get away from me you . . . faggot!" I remembered not to call him an s.o.b.

"Take it easy, Jack. Call me that again, and I'll really clean up with you."

"I wasn't . . ." I gripped the table leg and hoisted myself slowly. "I wasn't calling you that." My heart welled up. It was like I was trying to reach Kathy, and I was too helpless. "Oh, my God," I shouted, "I'm so sorry!" I began to cry.

"It's all right, Jack," he said. "I know it's just because of your condition!"

I scowled. "I'm not sorry about you. It's Kathy, poor Kathy, how much I hurt her even when I love her— I love her so much," I murmured; but I had enough presence of mind to regret saying it immediately. "Robert, are you my friend?"

"Yeah."

I swayed a little. "Then let's team up and help each other out and not tell anybody about our girls."

"All right," he said, and we shook hands. "We'll help each other and we won't tell anybody because that would be breaking the secret."

"You don't have to talk to me like I'm eight years old," I commanded. "*Goddamn* you." I went to the door. I could hear him laughing. I let myself imagine she was on the other side; when I opened it, she wasn't there, but then I had the feeling that she was close by. I went into the den. Robert followed me.

I picked up the phone. "Yes, you were right," I said. "You were right, after all. The only thing to do is call and get it over with."

He shrugged. "Maybe you should wait till tomorrow?"

"No. It's only eleven-thirty—she'll be up yet." I smiled. "I'm all right. Actually. What's so hard about a phone call? I just needed—this—to boost me."

"All right—call her up and get it over with."

I dialed her number happily and sat down in a big leather-stuffed chair.

Her number rang five times before her sister said, "Hello?"

"Hello, how are you, my sweet girl? Would you call your sister to the phone?"

She said yes and laid the receiver down. A minute later I heard it lift; she was back. "Who is this calling?"

"A good friend."

"Hello?" Kathy asked suddenly, and I was afraid. "Who is this?" Her voice was soft and very far away; I shuddered. "It's me, Jack. Look, I'm sorry. You know what for. I love you," I muttered. "I'll be seeing you tomorrow!"

She did not answer for a few seconds. "What's wrong with you? What's got into you to be doing something like this?"

"I'm sorry! For everything! Listen, my sweet . . ."

Her breathing was gone from the other end. I waited. "This is Kathy's father," a voice said. "What are you trying to pull anyway, you yellow-bellied son-of-a-bitch? If you come around here again, you'd better not let me see you first."

"No!" I said, tears springing to my eyes.

"Just you stay clear, that's all, and I mean it. I've got half a mind to call your parents. If you——"

I hung up.

7

We hitchhiked up to Westwood late in the afternoon and started walking to Mike MacKyntyre's house.

"I've been planning this a long time," Robert told me. "Ann's boy friend, he's some big monster and he looks like a Mongolian. He's also a senior and has a car. I can't beat that competition, so I always planned waiting till they screamed at each other."

"Are you sure they've screamed?"

"Oh yes. This guy at school told me. He thinks I talk to him because I like him. Actually, he's rather hideous, but he has friends who know Ann. So now I'm rushing in the gap with my tremendous appeal."

"Okay. Just remember not to pick on this guy MacKyntyre. He's very touchy and if he decides he doesn't like you, we won't get into the club tonight."

"What is this Chi-ro exactly?"

"It's a church club. They hold meetings in the basement cafeteria of a school. It lasts two hours—mainly you dance and talk and meet people. There're around two hundred members."

I hadn't seen Mike MacKyntyre in months. He was prissy, prudish, and treacherous; he always made me feel nervous because in some ways he was like me. He had been a guest at Kathy's party, sitting on the patio talking to a pretty blonde, and Robert had wanted to throw a firecraker at him.

His face was a web of wine-colored freckles, blotches through which peeped pink skin; his hair was an unnatural iron-gray and very thin and reminded me of the steel strands of a soap pad, but it was growing in quickly at the age of fifteen, and there was no trace of baldness.

"Come in!" he beamed, and I was sorry for what I had been thinking. He had never done me any harm, actually. He was shorter than I was and wearing mucklucks, and there was a cigarette slanted behind his freckled ear.

In his room a telescope stood in one corner. Twin beds took up most of the space, and a shelf of old, studious books by the window a little more. He lived on the ground floor of a duplex with his mother and sister. We talked briefly about this and that.

"How do you get women?" Robert asked suddenly.

Mac pondered. "I have no secrets."

"You must!"

"Are you trying to be funny?" He frowned and dismissed the subject. Reaching into a drawer, he brought out pictures he had taken of the moon; then he frightened us with stories about syphilis, and all the symptoms of syphilitic madness. Soon he grew careless about paying attention to whatever we might have to say and discussed himself and the things he had done or knew in a more and more rapid sequence of words. After a while I noticed Robert's eyes drifting to a photograph on the dresser of Mac's older sister. She was a blonde, intensely fair, with large bright eyes.

"My sister," Mac explained, catching the direction of his interest.

Robert crossed his legs, took a deep breath, exhaled with decisiveness. "When will she be home?"

"How should I know?"

"Well, I'll wait."

"You'll wait longer than you think!"

"How old is she?"

"Twenty-one."

"How old do you think I am?"

Mac scowled. "I don't know how old you are but you aren't old enough for my sister."

"What do you know about it?"

"Do you think you're an individualist?" Mac demanded. "You stand alone? You stand above everybody?"

"Yes, I'm tremendous."

"Well, that's a nice thing to think about yourself." He coughed. "Pardon me!"

Robert cleared his throat.

I coughed.

Mac laughed. "Huh, huh, huh! I coughed and you did, too. You both did. What individualists! Huh huh!"

"What do you call that?" I asked.

"Power of suggestion."

"Oh," Robert said, "is that when for instance if I slugged you—then Jack gets the same idea?" He grinned.

Mac scowled more darkly. "Yeah. Very funny. If you don't like it, you can leave, you know."

"I was kidding."

"Yeah!" He got up and stalked out of the door.

"Now you've done it," I said.

"What's with bald eagle and the gentle stories of sift?"

"Don't ever call him 'bald eagle.' "

"Why not?"

"He'd be rather perturbed and besides he can't help the hair on his head."

"Hair? You mean the Brillo cleansing pad?"

Mac came back to announce that we couldn't stay for dinner but that he'd meet us later at the Sunset Coffee Shop. I wondered if he really would, but there was not much to do but say yes, and we decided we might as well go and have something to eat there.

It took us about fifteen minutes to reach the hub of the village where the coffee shop was located. As we entered the big double door, I noticed a blond girl sitting alone at the counter, reading a newspaper. Robert recognized her as soon as I did. It was Ann. She was buxom and striking with a kind of athletic sensuality, a pretty face, cherubic-featured, and a little band of freckles on her nose.

We sat down in a booth where we could watch her. Robert told me wild stories about her physical strength, derived from the fact she had once knocked down a boy friend in grammar school.

"I don't believe it."

"It's true! Ask anybody!"

"All right."

"Now look at her!"

There was a cigarillo smoking in her ash tray.

"Where do you think she'll be going if she doesn't go to Chi-ro?" Robert asked.

"I don't know. Fruit maybe."

"Go fruit? What're you talking about?"

"She's smoking a cigarillo, isn't she? She knocked the guy down, didn't she? Didn't she?"

He thought it over. "I didn't know dames could go fruit."

"Well, they do."

"How?"

"I don't know how. Maybe she isn't one after all."

"I don't think she is one," he said. "How I hate her!"

"Why do you pick her out of all the others when she's so hard to make?"

"I didn't pick her out exactly. I don't know. I don't decide who I'll like in advance . . . You think she's a virgin, don't you?"

"I guess so."

"Of course she is!"

"All right," I submitted.

"*All right,* get up there!"

"Me?"

"If it was Kathy, don't you think I'd do the same? Break the ice and prepare for my tremendous coming."

I nodded. "I'll break the ice for your tremendous coming."

I got up slowly, went over to the counter, and sat down. I kept silent for a minute, then looked sideways at her casually, raised my eyebrows, and said, "Hi! How are you?"

She glanced up.

"You remember me," I said. "Kathy's old boy friend?"

She looked at me a minute with the startled blue eyes I could always remember her by. "Oh, yes. It's been a long time."

"How is Kathy these days?"

"I wouldn't know."

I looked over my shoulder at Robert. "Ann, you remember that guy sitting there, don't you?"

She followed my glance. Robert thought it meant I had prepared for his tremendous coming. He rose.

"No," she said, turning away, "who is he?"

"Don't you remember Robert?"

She looked around again and as she was doing so, he was sitting down on the stool next to her. She made a complete turn, saw him, leaned her elbows on the counter and stared straight ahead.

"Hi!"

She burst out laughing.

Robert scowled. "What's so funny?"

"Nothing," she said. "Mind telling me who you are?"

"What! Don't you remember Garrety—Ellie's party—as I walked in all the girls fainted?"

"Oh! Oh, yes."

"I phoned you later."

She smiled faintly.

"Put out the cigarillo," he said imperiously when she did not answer. "It bothers me."

"What?"

"I said, 'put it out.'" He reached over, picked it up, and crushed the glowing end in the ash tray.

"Just who do you think you are?"

"The prince."

"Trying to prove something, Prince?"

"You need me."

"Ha-ha! Tell me, who put you up to this?"

"No one, sorry! Let's get down to business: where are you going?"

"Right now I'm going crazy."

"I won't come along, you already have a head start on me, Crazy."

"Ha, ha!"

"Uh!" he mocked her.

She lapsed into a sullen silence. "Nobody tells me what to do, for your information."

"I tell you."

"No, you don't!" She picked up the dead cigarillo.

"I warn you not to light it," he said.

She raised her blond brows. "What would you do if I did?"

"If you really want to find out, go ahead."

"I will!" They tried to stare each other down. It was the most simple and childish thing. Robert and I always prided ourselves on our "princely" manner and much envied private vocabulary (which excluded common, infantile words like "cool" and "man" and "square") but here I found him trying this. I was trying to think of something that would break the deadlock when the street door opened behind us and a girl called, "Ann!"

Ann sighed and slid off the stool. "Be right with you, Debbie."

She took a wallet from her purse, got out twenty cents and laid it on the counter. But I was staring at the girl she had called Debbie. She stood there just inside the double glass doors, like a ballet dancer poised way up somewhere—with brunette hair down to her shoulders and large gray eyes. She was small and there was a lively excitement about her that was almost electric.

I heard Robert say, "See you at Chi-ro," and Ann reply, "Not if I see you first." Then both girls were gone, and I was aware of Mike MacKyntyre's scowling face pressed against the window. I had no idea of how long he had been staring at us, but from my first impression of his contorted features it might have been forever. The girls were climbing into a small green sedan already crowded with four or five others, when he turned and walked over to Ann.

Robert jumped up. "How does he know Ann, the idiotic bald eagle?"

We paid the bill and ran outside, but the small sedan was pulling out. Robert grabbed MacKyntyre's arm. "Hey—how do you know Ann?"

Mac raised his eyebrows. "I have classes with her. Why?"

"What did you say to her just now?"

"I asked how she was doing with her homework. Why, what's it to you?"

"It's nothing to me! How did you get here so fast anyway?"

"My sister gave me a ride."

We went back inside and ordered hamburgers. Mac told us he had gone to grammar school with Ann, and three or four years ago she had caught polio and had become a tennis player in redeveloping herself.

"She should be nice to me," Robert said. "The charity. I'm a great contributor. I went down to the beach once and I saw all these limping people swimming, so I gave a penny."

"You shouldn't talk that way," Mac muttered.

"Why don't you shut up? I'll tell you what I'll do with her.

I'll challenge her to a game of chess and the intelligence will be beating me, so I'll have to let her win. Then I'll box with her and be carried out on a stretcher. But then we'll go up to her room and I'll win that one. Hah!"

Mac looked concerned. "Maybe you think you're free to try all that. Well——"

"I know all about her boy friend. They screamed at each other, and now he's in the hospital and can't move."

"Is that so?" He sipped his ice water with a brooding expression.

I tried to shut Robert up, but he kept on and on about Ann and what he would 'do.' When we were halfway through dinner, Mac said he just remembered he had forgotten to tell his mother when he'd be home. I was suspicious, but Robert didn't seem to notice anything wrong. Mac stayed in the booth a little longer than two minutes; he left the door open and now and then looked back at us almost bitterly.

Walking down to Wilshire, he more or less ignored us until one of Robert's remarks solidified his defensiveness, and he began talking about his great good friend. I would like this friend, he said, because he was like me. We were—all of us except Robert—rowdy intellectuals.

He seemed to wish praise for originating the term, but I held back any that might have occurred to me. I had no intention of joining a band headed by him known as "The Rowdy Intellectuals."

"I've got a letter here," he went on, reaching in his back pocket, "from my friend. It's the funniest damn thing you've ever read."

I stopped under a street lamp and read the letter. It started out, "Goddamn you," and got even funnier.

We agreed it was hilarious. Robert caught my eye, and I burst out laughing.

Mac turned to me with a grin. "Delayed action, huh?"

He was too much.

8

In the church basement that served for the club's meeting place, we met a few friends, quieted down while the priest made a speech, and said a prayer with him. Then we began to wait. After half an hour Ann still hadn't arrived, so to kill time we wandered around. Robert began dancing with a Mexican girl named Melinda, and I cut in on him. We were each other's competition; I panned him, and he panned me, but later on I praised him to a little girl named Janet, mainly because I couldn't see her myself. All this time we were watching the door and hardly caring.

"What time is it?" Robert finally asked during an intermission.

I looked at my watch. "A quarter of nine."

"Do you think the girls are ever going to come?" he asked.

And suddenly Debbie was there, framed in the entrance, glancing around brightly. Ann was behind her, and at Ann's side, an arm around her shoulders, was a tall, pale young man with small eyes, high, pointed cheek bones and lank brown hair. His face had a slight Mongolian cast; he was lean, but his arms were long and sinewy and his hands big and powerful. Ann was flushed, happy, and excited, and when her eyes met his, they lingered overlong.

Robert stared at them balefully. "The Mongolian boy friend. There's a knife in my back," he muttered. "Somebody panicked this Fred."

I shrugged. "Maybe Ann told him about you."

"Like hell."

"Are you thinking what I'm thinking?"

He nodded. "The bald eagle Mac, who flies above the city searching for a mouse to devour."

"Remember him making a phone call?"

"Naturally. Who else could it be? Because why should Ann be so anxious to get the monster back? She'd play the field a bit before beckoning with her little finger and feeling the rush of wind on her face as he comes charging."

I sighed. "So what'll we do to Mac?"

He hesitated with a dark face. "We could pound him to the dust, but then do you know what would happen?"

"He'd tell, is that what you mean?"

"Yes, slightly. He'd tell the Mongolian, and then there'd be a big rumpus."

"So what're you going to do now?"

"I'll throw some *bull* at the bald eagle, who jealously searches kitchen sinks for the Brillo pad to put on his head."

"How're you going to do this?"

"I'll tell him I hate her. And give him messages to transmit, so she won't forget me." He gazed at the couple with brooding eyes.

"Why don't you just go over and ask her for a dance? What's so hard about that?"

"I'm afraid not! Do you know what would happen? They'd

tell her how old I am, that I have no car, and hate opera and all that. No! I don't want her to know me, I just want to take advantage of her, you know—slip in like I nearly did tonight before a thousand traitorings."

"You might have to wait a pretty long time."

"She'll get tired. He ain't like I am, he'll always come running as she calls him—but I'll only, well, I'll never come *running*: oh, never run. I'll only be around when I feel like it. I don't want her except if I can have her my own way . . . Him! How can she want somebody who'll never leave? How hideous!"

"But he *did* leave."

"He also came running back. You know, I think I *will* ask her for this dance." He jerked my hand. "Shake. We team to beat the women who are throwing hatreds. Now's the time to tell her about the Mongolian idiot who sits on his pony shooting arrows and following Attila; and also about the bald eagle snatching a mouse in the night and beating his wings over the phone. I need you to help me."

"How?"

He released his hand and put it on my shoulder. "I want you to ask Debbie to dance as I rush Ann."

"Why?"

"They'll all look at you and think, 'Oh, he's too shy! He's brought his friend for moral support.' A thousand deceptions."

"And some fears."

"I'm not afraid."

I was very dubious but we quickly cut through the crowd to the corner where Ann and her friends were sitting on chairs along the wall. There were ten or twelve of them, and they were talking back and forth with all the enthusiasm of a school clique. When we stopped in front of them, the hubbub diminished somewhat, but when we continued to stand there, they looked out at us with hostility from their little private world. It almost gave me the feeling I was back trying to crash Kathy's party.

"I'm waiting, Ann," Robert said.

She flushed with surprise. "You want to dance?"

"What else? Come on!"

Fred swung his long arm off the rim of Ann's chair; his expression grew concerned and then went into a scowl. Ann glanced at him and settled back hesitantly.

In desperation I smiled at Debbie, who was watching us with glowing, amused eyes. "Can I have this dance?" I asked. She looked at me for a moment longer—a look that went deeper than I thought could ever have been possible; then she shrugged and rose to her feet gracefully.

I pulled her toward me although the girl is supposed to precede you to the dance floor. Out of the corner of my eye I could see Robert bringing Ann to her feet almost forcibly.

Debbie never completely merged while we danced, as though she were obliged to stand apart, belong to no one, and be noticed by all. She was even smaller than I had estimated her to be, in the doorway of the Sunset coffee shop. In fact it was almost embarrassing that the top of her head did not reach higher than my shoulder. But when it came down to that, her pretty face, her long hair, the wildness of her gray eyes, and the symmetry of her body compensated. She danced very well, so well that I had to check myself from habitually distrusting her; she made me aware of my own clumsiness, yet I did not ever seem to interfere with her own movement. It made me think of all the dancing classes I had gone to under the direction of Miss Dunne, where we were taught to be polite and perform incomprehensible steps with girls in starched dresses, serving them punch afterwards and being sure always to never disturb the white handkerchief in the breast pocket of our blue suits.

I wished now I hadn't despised the classes so thoroughly, not so much because I would have been a better dancer but because I wanted to complement her—Debbie.

"I'm Jack," I said.

"I know who you are."

"Who am I?"

"You're the boy in the coffee shop," she laughed. She had no difficulty in looking up, since there was space between us. "Do you know who I am?"

"Debbie."

She looked at me very deeply again as if she was searching for something, something tremendous that would make me rate. She seemed to expect something of me, but I was not sure what it was. I had an inkling then that girls made up their minds about boys as quickly as boys made up theirs about girls, but I didn't know how to help her. I had the feeling I knew a great deal about her, and that she knew me, too, all except the specific history, but I didn't know how to deal with her. I had a tendency to freeze up even when I wanted to become more personal. I wished I was seventeen instead of her own age, if I had been seventeen, we would have been equals.

"Are you coming here next week?"

"I don't know," she said. "I might have a rehearsal."

"A rehearsal? For what?"

"A play. I'm an actress."

"Oh." I thought a minute. "A Hollywood actress?"

"No," she laughed, "I'll have to wait a few years for that."

"Where do you act now?" I said.

"In school. Drama school. Last year I won a scholarship."

"For acting?"

"Uh-huh."

"Good."

"And what do *you* do?"

"I do nothing. Hell, I'm only fifteen."

"I'm fourteen." I didn't know whether she felt inferior or superior to me, but for the time being I banked on a feeling of inferiority.

The record came to a close. "Do you want to dance some more?"

"I think I'd better get back," she said.

"Well, I'll be here next week," I said, "even if I have to walk again. Damn busted axle."

She smiled.

"Why don't I give you a ring to find out if you're coming?" I asked.

She hesitated a few agonizing seconds. "I wouldn't know until the last minute, but my number is Arizona one-three-seven-two-four."

I had gotten Kathy's number at the close of a dance, too; the prefixes were even the same. I kept repeating it to myself. Phone numbers of new girls—they always seemed to me like the combinations of love, although I rarely got beyond the mere numbers.

I walked Debbie halfway back to her clique, then looked around for Robert. I saw him standing still and talking earnestly with Ann, even though the next dance had begun. I glanced around, trying to spot Melinda, but before I could find her, Robert caught up with me alone.

"I gotta find Mac!" he said.

"Why?"

"There isn't much time left to string him."

"Wait . . . there he is."

Mac, his hair looking more like a steel soap pad than ever under the unshaded lights, was with a friend at the far end of the hall. As we came up, the boy wandered away. Robert began talking warmly about Ann and Fred and gradually convinced Mac he had been wrong in his suspicions. He even suggested that Mac play a little joke—that he tell Ann Robert liked her a little. This was very funny. Mac laughed and after some prodding consented.

"Do you want to go some place after Chi-ro?" I asked.

He turned a little red, his eyes melting behind the glasses he was wearing now. "I'm afraid I can't. Someone—is giving me a ride."

"Who's that?"

"Oh, a friend of mine." He looked at us. "As a matter of fact, it's Ann's boy friend, Fred."

"Oh, is it?" Robert said politely. "Well, give him my regards, will you? I think he's a real cat."

"Sure!"

"Cigarette, Mac?" I asked. You could sneak a smoke in the rear of the hall if you confined it to a few drags.

"No," he said, "I can't." He grew sad. He seemed to want

to tell us the story of his life. He described how he wanted to be a celestial navigator and how when he was twelve he had had a chance to hump a girl and of course he hadn't known what it was all about. He went to public school now with Debbie and Ann, but when he had been going to ours, I remembered he used to wear a gray army cap to hide his hair. So I let myself feel a little sad, too. But Robert kept a straight face.

"You sure you don't want a cigarette?" I asked.

"I can't."

"You used to smoke three packs a day last year!"

He shook his head. "Ever heard of nicotine poisoning?"

"What does it mean?" Robert demanded.

"What does it sound like?" He held out his hand. The top joints of the middle and index fingers were stained a dirty yellow. "The doctor told me if I started to smoke again, I could die in a few months. I get more smoke intentionally blown in my face." He smiled, but then the smile went out and his eyes grew moist again on the wave of a memory. "I hate it . . . it's so natural to light up—and you know you're going to die. I wouldn't care if only somebody else didn't care. But when somebody else does care—that's what makes you get real afraid at night."

"Your girl?"

The memory and the tears receded. "Sure!"

He took out his wallet and showed me her picture. She was horrible.

We nodded.

He put it back. "I'll be seeing you guys."

"Take care of yourself," I said.

He moved off.

"The poor little eagle," Robert said. "Running around with

old letters in his pocket, poisoned and weeping always. Too bad he's so idiotic or I'd feel sorry for him."

"Did you tell Ann what he did?"

"Yes. I was very casual. The way I said it made them sound like punks. I said, 'I thought you'd like to know.' She said, 'Thanks!' How about that. Did you get anywhere with Debbie?"

"She gave me her phone number."

"Good. Then you can ask her questions about Ann and transmit messages. What's the matter?"

I grew more gloomy. "By rights you owe me a favor."

He stared at me blankly. "Okay, how do you want me to help you?"

I dropped down in a chair. "You told me once Kathy's sister liked you."

He nodded.

"I'll pay your way to a movie," I said.

"With her?"

"C'mon, agree to it," I said, offering my hand. "All you have to do is have her meet you this Saturday afternoon. I'll be there and we'll recruit her as a spy for me."

"Do I have to make out with her?"

"It isn't the worst thing anybody ever asked you to do."

He hesitated, then we shook hands.

When the meeting ended, we went outside with the crowd. Robert spotted Ann, her boy friend, and Mac walking off toward the parking lot, and we followed from a distance.

He leaned against the fender of a parked Chevy and watched as they got into a white, dagoed Ford sedan. Ann was laughing at something and her laughter carried clear in the chill night air. He winced. Fred backed up his car, then tore out. Robert threw away his cigarette and walked toward the lot exit, the way they had gone.

"I feel like I dreamed this once, sometime," he said. "Like I always knew I'd have to take my girl away from somebody else who was an idiot."

"Yeah?"

He stopped and looked at me. "Do you think it's so hideous to be a . . . a . . . what you called me last night?"

"No— I'm sorry I ever said it."

He turned and kept on walking. "I'm glad Ann doesn't know I'm *that,* right now. I'm glad she doesn't know—but some day I'm going to tell her. I wish I knew *what* to tell her —when I tell her."

"Maybe you *should* ask your father."

"Of course! 'Daddy, am I your untrue son? What went on that night, O Dads?' Of course! All that would happen would be that he'd throw me out. Or he'd never speak to me. If he thought I knew it—it's all right if he knows it—he'd hate me. Of course, he already does hate me, but I can take the current hatred, it just flares up now and then."

"Sorry I mentioned it."

"It isn't his fault that I happened along, and if I blamed him we'd probably never be able to live together again. But I don't blame you for mentioning it. You can't help the tremendous idiotness."

"The word is 'idiocy.'"

"'Idiotness' sounds better."

"Why don't you spread your wings, birdie?" I demanded.

"I'll spread them if you guide me to Ann's house and drop

me on her bed, so I can put my thing in her—then she'd be mine—always and forever like when you get married."

"You think so?"

"I know it." He lit a cigarette. "It'll take a long time before I get her. I hope it doesn't take too long." He shrugged. "I'd really go batty then, I really would, you know that?"

9

Although we plotted over them constantly, our loves, or our obsessions with them, did not prevent other romances. It was too early in life for monogamy. I had no idea what monogamy really meant, and I wouldn't have been predisposed to follow it even if Kathy were my girl friend; it did seem to me, though, that if I were interested enough in a girl, I would be too busy with her to search out other girls. We had no conception of abstract loyalty. Most necking did not even include romance, so it mattered even less.

He made the date with Carol on Friday night. Her mother would drive her to the matinee, and Carol would meet a school friend inside. He was the friend.

The matinee was attended mostly by little children; the last time I had gone to the movies on a Saturday afternoon I had been one of them, and I had forgotten what it was like. They screamed, chattered, ran up and down the aisles, fought, cried, threw tantrums, spilled soft drinks, and bounced up and down in their seats. Even in all the commotion, Carol couldn't miss Robert on an aisle seat looming very tall in the midst of the children; I sat, hunching over, in the row behind them.

She was late.

She came gliding down the steps so swiftly that the first I actually saw of her she was already squeezing past Robert.

"Carol! Where were you?"

She sat down, shifting away from him as if to show she still would have to be won over. "My mother had errands. How have you been?"

"Depressed."

"Oh?" she asked, fixing her eyes on him intently.

The children were deathly silent. The enemy in the war picture was coming again. Bang! Bang! Bang!

"Hello," I said, leaning my head between their shoulders.

She gave a little scream.

"What are you doing here?"

"I'm his friend; I want to be yours; I've come to talk to you," I said.

The tension had lifted on the screen, and the children were chattering and running up and down. Carol, rigid, turned around and speculated over me through the dark. She had very soft, thick, brown hair; her nose was broad, her eyes large, and her lips full. She had a child's prettiness. She was very young in fact. Her unreal breasts were two sharp points against her sweater.

"What do you want to talk to me about?"

"I'll tell you. I've always liked you," I said, "and felt you were someone I could trust. Really. Robert's nuts about you. So why don't you give me some details about your sister?"

"Why?"

"Because I like her."

She smiled haughtily. "She doesn't like you!"

"Forget about that."

"Ha!" she said. "You called me a 'dear thing' over the phone. You're crazy!"

"Won't you do this for me?" I asked. "Haven't I always been your friend, your big brother? Why don't you talk to me about Kathy, and tell me things about her from time to time? C'mon now, listen."

"Ha, ha!"

"Listen!" I grabbed her wrist.

She screamed.

The usher ran down, waving his flashlight.

"Are you molesting this girl?" he demanded, the light pouring on Robert's startled face.

"No," Carol pouted. "I just despise this one sitting in back, that's all."

He shifted the light to me, held it there for a second, then switched it off and marched back up the steps. A child came running past him, laughing and screaming and juggling a cup of soft drink. Another child was chasing him. Robert stuck out his foot and the second child went flying, seemed to find his feet before he hit, and without even breaking stride, kept laughing and screaming, and, hurling his popcorn like stones.

"Carol," I said, leaning forward again. "Be a good girl—c'mon now . . ."

She shook her head coldly and turned away.

"Goddamn it!"

"Um!" she said in a shocked whisper, as if she knew it was all true now what they had been saying about me.

"Carol!" Robert broke in. "You're so gorgeous and your adulthood beats me and I have these dreams about you at night and the beauty is flowing everywhere. O love! And so do me a favor. I have this curiosity about this dame because I'm studying old fossils. She was at the party where I met you– Oh, forever, and the gorgeousness of it, and we'll inhabit the cottage covered with hideous vines with the children weeping—my other children. But tell me if you know her —Ann Fields?"

"I guess I know her," she said, bug-eyed at his outburst.

"How well do you know her? Very well?"

"Why?"

"Oh, Carol, you're so little and your mind is, too, and you think all little thoughts, and you know all little people, and everything you do is little. And Ann must seem like a giant to you, but tell me what you know about her anyway—and don't ask why because you're too little to understand."

"I'm never going to tell you!"

"Then you may get out, O hideous one."

She stood up angrily.

"No, stay, Carol; you're so gorgeous!"

She bent over and I heard her gasp.

"*Don't,*" Robert said. "Don't cry, Carol. I didn't mean it. I was only kidding. Sit down." She tried to get past him, and he trapped her just as she made the aisle. "Where are you going? C'mere!"

"Let go of me!" she cried.

"All right," he said. "I'm letting go. Don't weep! Why does everybody we know weep? Please! Carol!" he shouted as she started up the steps.

I sprang in front of her like a hero.

"I'm your friend," I said. "Don't cry."

"You're a mani-*ac!*" she screamed.

Children began screaming all around us.

Robert and I rushed past her for the door; the flashlight glared in our eyes.

"There's a mad monster running around down there!" Robert shouted.

The usher sped past us. We broke into the foyer, leapt down the staircase, and ran outside. The sun was bright and hot, the afternoon was mellow. We didn't slow down until we hit Wilshire.

I often thought about Debbie when we were sitting in some dark, rundown bowling alley in Hollywood, or trying to pick up a girl in a show. I remembered her eyes, her light gray, long-lashed eyes as they looked into mine, trying to find something there I had not been able to find for her. That was the way I always remembered her.

Because she never came to the club again.

I used to phone. Either she was out or unable to speak with me, or she could speak but only for a minute, and finally I gave up calling altogether—over Robert's objections. Soon she became unreal in my memory.

But Melinda was real. I became her casual boy friend at Chi-ro. I loved her sweaters; she wore nothing but violet sweaters. Her mouth was very soft, ripe, and red; her eyes were dreaming and brown, lazy, languorous eyes. We almost never smiled at each other, almost never spoke. She was a ninth grader. Janet was, too. Janet became "Gar's gal"—in practically the same way Melinda belonged to me. She was a five-foot-two with large, friendly brown eyes and a merry, cutely shaped mouth. She always seemed to be wearing white sweaters.

Robert spoke no more than a few words to Ann each time she came to Chi-ro, and sometimes I caught a glimpse of him watching her out of a shadow. She did not come every week, though. And even when she did, Fred was with her and they would stay only a short while. But the last two Wednesdays in April she was alone and remained the whole evening, a dreamy look on her face . . . her eyes wandering around the room, a little thoughtful, a little bored. She seemed expectant, waiting; it was spring again, and perhaps spring had always brought with it something new.

We ran into her and some of her girl friends one Wednesday evening waiting for the basement door to open. They were at the bottom of a short flight of stairs, and we stood over the well, leaning against the guard rail. She looked around and up at us and smiled with amusement.

"One of you have a cigarette?"

Robert pulled out a pack of Pall Malls and hung it over her head.

She mounted the steps. "Thank you," she said.

"You can owe me the penny."

"That's very kind of you."

He struck a match. She bent her head so close to me I could smell the natural oils of her thick, clean, short-cut blond hair. His hand trembled as he held the match to her cigarette, and she had to dart it after the flame for five or six seconds before she could draw. While she was still taking the light, she looked up at him inquisitively with her innocent, startled blue eyes, and their close-up effect made him flinch.

"What's the matter?"

"Nothing."

"Robert," she said, "Robert . . ." It was magic, as if you had been wandering through a crowd of strangers and suddenly found someone enchanted, put under a spell, someone you'd hardly ever spoken to. She was full of discovery, surprised into laughter, overjoyed. He kept a tight expression so to say, locking it in, lips thrust out, but a sparkle in his eyes.

"Robert, do you . . . ?"

He leaned over the railing. "Where's your boy friend—is he still out following Attila and beating Pope Leo?"

"I don't know where he is. He isn't out following Attila, though."

"Well, good. Why don't you never find out where he is again?"

"I never have to find out where he is."

"I know. He tells you, doesn't he? He returns with the leash in his mouth. Not like some people."

"Which are they?"

"Princely people like me."

"Oh, oh."

"Yes, people who are a thousand suedes like me, beating all the women with the ermine trailing on the floor, and never telling."

"Everybody tells."

"Oh, I never tell because they're so many I keep forgetting."

"Once you phoned me."

"Yes, I phoned you, and we spoke for an instant."

"It was something like two hours."

"Some short stretch of time like that."

She nodded. "Garrety. Robert Garrety."

"Yes, but I use so many pen names, I keep forgetting all the time."

"You mean aliases."

"Of course. The aliases are everywhere. I hear you lift weights for your figure."

"No, I don't."

"Then you think you can play tennis and you run around leaping over nets."

She smiled. "Don't you have a girl friend here? A freshman?"

The word 'freshman' caught him up a little. "I don't remember exactly. You mean college freshman? And how's Moss?" he added, "I never see him any more."

"Moss?"

"MacKyntyre, you know, the *betrayer*. With the growth on his head."

"I don't know how he is. But why is he a betrayer?"

He laughed. "Remember? That night I told you about the phone call?"

"Oh. So he's a betrayer! And you——"

"Yes," Robert said, looking down at the girls. "Has he died yet?"

"No, he hasn't died yet."

"He promised he would."

Below the doors opened.

"Are you coming?" she said.

"No, I'll see you inside."

The other girls went in.

"So he betrayed you?"

"Slightly."

"What had you been planning?"

"Oh, sorry, you'll never know."

"Won't you tell?"

"Sometime I'll show you. All right?"

She smiled and went down the steps into the club. Robert slumped on the railing.

"How did I do?"

"Fine—you did fine."

"How did I sound—lousy?"

"You sounded fine."

"I couldn't even barely light her cigarette. What did I do wrong?"

"Nothing."

He stared down at the well, his arms hanging in mid-air. "You're telling the truth, aren't you?"

"Yeah."

"Shake!"

We shook hands, partly to convey my convictions, partly to seal our union in his enterprise.

It was all very indefinite. Ann kept shifting back and forth, changing her mind—so he danced with her as infrequently as possible. He didn't want to be particularly noticed because he didn't want her judgment of him to be influenced by her friends. But he did learn that Debbie planned to spend tomorrow night at Ann's house because the following day,

Friday, most of the tenth grade was going to ditch classes to go to the beach. And Ann's parents would be out.

"Can Jack and I drop over tomorrow night?" he asked.

She shrugged. "I don't know. Why don't you call me first?"

That was the way he kept telling it to me all the way home.

10

The next afternoon we had an early dinner at my house, bummed up to Westwood, and went to the coffee shop. He was very exact about wanting to phone from a place that reminded him of her. It wasn't dark yet; we waited. He bought a vial of mouth-sweetener, and now and then drank a little. We had coffee and watched college students from UCLA wander in and out.

I laid my head on my arms, and he sang a little stanza softly to himself:

"Oh, the monkey wrapped his tail
Around the flagpole
To see the grass grow
Around his—hole"

"Why don't you shut up?" I asked, raising my head. "You want to be thrown out of here? When are you going to call Ann anyway?"

He shrugged. "I'm debating it. There's a right time to call and a wrong time."

"Are you kidding?"

"No. I gotta catch her in a certain mood, you see."

"So are you going to sit here and figure out the mood she's in?"

"When I feel like calling her, she should be ready to say yes. When it's dark enough, and I feel like I waited around long enough—that'll be when."

"What if she still isn't in the mood?"

"If she isn't in it by that time, I'll be tremendously in it. And I can convince her."

"Couldn't you convince her to let us come over now?"

"No, I just explained. This isn't the right time for me. I feel lousy."

I lowered my head on my arms. "I don't believe it will depend on her mood, anyway."

"Everything depends on people's moods. Everything! Probably the only reason I was born was because of some mood."

"I doubt it."

"You're wrong." He stared at me searchingly, then leaned forward, his hand tight around a glass. "I ain't trying to . . . what?"

"Justify."

"Yes. I don't know enough about it." He seemed to choke a minute, tears flashed in his eyes. "I'm just saying that you can understand these things somewhat. There's a lot of things I don't know; like why I'm living with untrue father; I don't know why he'd want me."

"I know."

"All right! Forget about it!" He sprawled back. "What time is it now, anyway?"

"Six-thirty."

"We'll call her in five minutes."

In five minutes he phoned and she said, yes, that we could drop over if we felt like it.

"All right, we'll be there within nine hours or so."

But he took the distance to Wilshire in a fast trot.

We hitchhiked a good two miles up Vista Canyon, got off at a major intersection, and started walking up Riverglen, her street, which was carved out of a steep mountainside. It was very bucolic in the growing darkness; there were no sidewalks; dogs barked at us constantly. A car came around a bend, dazzling us with its bright lights, and as it rolled past us slowly, we saw a couple inside.

Robert burst out laughing. "Her father! It was her father and mother—leaving!" He went on more quickly, "I knew it would happen. All I had to do was wait for it. But now it's going to happen, we have to be tremendous. We have to make up for the fact we can't be regular boy friends running around in a car and asking parents if it's all right to smoke in their hideous presence."

I frowned. "I used to be a *boy friend,* except I didn't have any car. There's nothing wrong in asking parents if you can smoke."

"Except that I'd do it anyway, so there wouldn't be much point in asking. What do the parents care about it? What have they ever done but run around in a bedroom and then raise the kid they're stuck with? Should I be an idiotic gentleman because they think they're so tremendous with legal humping and the children streaming out always? I have four parents of my own, and they don't send me."

"They're just people!"

"They're not people when they act like parents. The old

fogies always thinking, 'What do you want to do with my little girl?' Their little girl is as big as I am!"

"This girl is. Some of the ones you know aren't."

"I've never done a girl wrong. I'm so nice."

"But you've tried to do wrong."

"Naturally, everybody tries."

"You're just mad at her parents because you're younger than she is, and they wouldn't approve."

"That's another thing," he said. "We can't tell anybody about this because if it got around she might faint. That doesn't bother me. She knew I couldn't be like the Mongolian following Attila. How tremendous I succeeded anyway!"

"Maybe," I said. "We haven't even gotten in yet!"

"Shut up, why don't you?" he answered. "Don't you think I know that? Do I look very calm and merry? I got marked down for three F's in three different classes today. God—right now I feel like running back down to Vista and not stopping. Do you feel that way?"

"Not very much."

"That's because you don't care very much."

"I wish you cared a little less with your raving hysterics."

We rounded the bend. Her street was dark, lonely, and peaceful; through the trees we could see people moving past lighted windows. The moon was growing yellow, and a frail wind was shaking the leaves. We reached her place.

"Stop," he said.

I opened the split-rail gate.

"Stop!"

"We're here!" I said.

He grabbed my arm and pulled me back behind a tree. "Will you take it easy? Stay here a minute."

"What's wrong with you? Why do I have to stay here?"

"Because I said so."

"Drop dead!"

"Gladly." He leaned his arm on the tree, leaned his head on his arm, and watched her house. "Just wait a minute. I don't feel right about it again."

"Are you going to tell me we have to wait till she gets in the *mood?*"

"No. I just have to think." He straightened up suddenly. "Okay. I'm ready."

He had finally made me nervous. "All right, go on," I said.

He opened the gate, and I followed him up to the door. He knocked three times. I slunk into a shadow cast by a trellis toward the side.

The door opened. Light struck his face. I saw breasts bulging softly in a black sweater—then Ann's blond hair, her inquiring expression.

"All right, I'm here! Dry the eyes!" Robert said and stormed in.

"I'm also here," I said, following. "Hello!"

He strode into the foyer, down a few shallow steps to the living room. "Start mixing, I'll take Vodka."

"I don't live here," a voice said.

It was Debbie. She looked small on the couch; she held a book on her lap, and she had on a pleated white blouse and red pedal pushers; her hair fell softly to her shoulders.

Near the fireplace, a portable phonograph was playing "Sing Sing Sing."

Robert stopped behind a sofa, glancing all around as if fighting temptations to efface himself by going to the bar, or to the French doors that led outside, or by sitting down quietly in a chair. He was growing red in the face.

"Make yourself right at home," Ann said. "How are you, Robert?"

"Depressed. Why don't you get something good on the phonograph?"

"Help yourself."

The black sweater moved alongside me. "You remember Debbie, don't you?" There was a blank where my name should have been.

"Jack," I supplied, feeling crushed.

Debbie wriggled her shoulders a little and discarded the book. Nobody said anything else. I stood there, smiling a little.

It was a large living room, letting out to a terrace through French doors. The carpet, furniture, walls, and drapes were in somber colors; suspended between the two matching sofas was a sunburst chandelier, scattering small squares of light over the floor. Robert, hovering over the phonograph, dropped the needle on the turntable, jammed an LP into place, and almost tore the automatic arm out of the socket before Ann could grab the operation away from him.

"I'm getting it!" he said, staring at her darkly.

She shook her head. "What record do you want to hear?"

"It doesn't matter! Forget it. Let's go outside."

She raised her eyebrows. "It's cold outside."

"It's also lonely. C'mon!"

He pulled her out the French doors. After a moment, I walked over, put on a record, and then sat down beside Debbie. She stared straight ahead, saying nothing. "How's the acting?" I threw my arm around the rim of the sofa.

She shrugged. "Well, I haven't been offered the starring role in a picture yet."

"I'll see if I can manage some pull."

"Yes, see about it, will you?"

"I hear you're ditching school tomorrow. That's very bad."

"You seem to have ideas on the subject."

"Right. I'm full of ideas. I'm a good boy with bad ideas, but some people can't tell the difference."

"Why?"

"Because what's good to some people is bad to others. Like your eyes I keep on remembering, they're good. Ask me about other parts of your body."

She flared up. "I ought to hit you."

"Try it."

"How old did you once say you were?"

"I was sixteen three weeks ago."

"I had a birthday, too, by the way. I'm fifteen now." I knew she hadn't forgotten. "How old is your friend?"

"Seventeen."

"I don't believe it!"

"He looks seventeen, doesn't he?"

"In a way."

I leaned closer. "He is."

"*She* has her doubts," she said, "and so . . . do I." Our lips met after an awful, trembling, giddy hesitation. But we were wooden and stiff. Her lips were very light and sweet, but my eyes were open and after a few seconds hers flickered open, too. So we had to stop. She raised her eyebrows sharply. "Don't get any ideas."

I was taken aback, hurt, and disappointed. "Anything you say."

Robert and Ann returned. He did not look happy. Ann shivered and sat down across from us. The girls began talking to each other about school; Robert and I said practically nothing.

Finally Robert wandered over to the bar; the girls were laughing now over everything; it was all impenetrable, I felt they would go into shrieks if I said a word. Then Ann suddenly looked somewhere behind me.

"What are you doing?" she asked.

I turned to see Robert mixing drinks haphazardly.

"Who said you could do that?" she demanded.

"Nobody. I happen to feel like it."

I felt very strange. It was as if nothing had been accomplished over the long months we had waited. They were arguing just like the first time I had seen them together. Our visit tonight was a mistake, a fraud.

"Some people have a nerve," Debbie said.

He scowled at her. "Oh, shut up, you hideous midget. You may get out! Good riddance."

"You shut up!" Ann cried, jumping to her feet.

He walked over and shoved a drink in her hand. "Make me."

"I ought to throw this at you!"

"You'd get mine right back."

"You'd do it, wouldn't you?"

"I'd also knock you down!"

She took a step back, watching him carefully. "You really would?"

"Yes, to hurt myself for the things I've done."

She pondered, then asked softly, "Is it always like this, Robert?"

"Never."

"Ha!" Debbie said loudly.

"Debbie, you look all right and the eyes attract, but quit interrupting."

He seemed to have given Ann an impression of what his abuse was really all about. She wasn't angry any more. "Never in your life?"

"Until now. That's what I was trying to tell you outside. I shout at you, and it hurts me. I'd knock you down, and it would kill me. Some things don't hurt. I wish we'd get around to them. I've been waiting to get around to them for a long time. I could tell you a lot of stories."

"I'd like to hear."

"Oh, stories about waiting, getting angry, feeling very sad, not getting to sleep at night. About dreaming too much. Hideous stories."

"Why?"

"Too much time passes, and nothing is accomplished."

"How much time?"

He emptied half the glass. "I don't know. Why do you care?"

"I just do."

"Am I supposed to fall at your feet?"

She sipped her drink. "No. You're very strange, do you know that?"

"You're hardly worthy of me, do you know that?"

"Is that so?"

"That's what I like to think."

She sat down on the sofa, and he dropped down beside her. He finished his drink and held the glass out to me; I took it to the bar, then stood there looking at the array of bottles on the glass shelves. Scotch, rye, vodka, gin, Benedictine, cognac. I put some of each into a pitcher, filled it with soda, and poured fresh drinks for everyone.

Ann barely glanced at me as I handed her the glass. "Why didn't I know all this time?" she was saying.

"You weren't looking," Robert told her.

"Maybe I was looking, though."

He took her hand and pressed it tightly. "No, you weren't. You were in Attila's camp. You were going to go to Rome to beat the Pope. I was waiting. I read history, I knew you were never going to get into Rome. But you thought you were. Damn you."

"Who's Attila?" Debbie asked.

"Will you go to hell?" he said.

"I'll never understand you," Ann said.

He was almost feverish with the things he had been wanting to say for so long. "I'll never understand *you.* I waited too long. I waited so long I don't even want to understand you any more."

"What a dumb sweet couple," Debbie said after a hiccough which made her look around in surprise.

"Was it that long?" Ann asked.

He sipped at his drink. "It ain't over yet."

"Not over? Why?"

"I'm telling you all about it, that doesn't mean it's over. It ain't over the second you walk in the door, or when you hold hands"—he raised their locked hands—"how stupid to hold hands. How hideous—little boys and girls holding hands like they're afraid they might wander away from each other: what a tragedy. Shed tears." He broke their clasp.

"What do you want me to do?" she asked, leaning against him.

"For what reason?"

"So that I can show I want to be close to you . . . affectionate."

"I can get a dog to be affectionate."

"And would you feel the same way toward him?"

"No," Robert said.

"I'm glad for that."

He put his arms around her, and as if overwhelmed with the feel of her body, the scent of her hair, her firm, yielding breasts underneath the sweater, he kissed her cheek and glided softly up to her ear.

"How inspiring," Debbie said to me now. She hiccoughed again and reacted with the same surprise. "Could I trouble you for a remedy?"

"Yeah." I leaned over to kiss her but she turned away. I grunted.

"Am I disgusting to you?" she asked, turning back. Then through my own haze I knew she was high.

"No, I like you."

She considered me a moment solemnly. "You know, you *are* sweet."

"Oh, he just *is*," Robert said, fastening his attention on us. "But haven't you gotten out yet?"

"Why don't you shut up," I put in, "you maniac?"

"Yes," Debbie said, "leave us alone!"

"All right, let's do it!" Robert said. "Let's go." He drew Ann's mouth to his suddenly and kept it a long time, and she lost all rigidity, her body seeming to melt into his with passion and the shock of ecstasy, as if her kisses had always been cheap before. She was breathless and bright-eyed. They drew apart. "A thousand rushes," he said, "as we beat other rooms." He met her eyes and for once, at least, he found an understanding. "Do you want me to say it? Do you want to hear it? In front of them? In front of everybody? I've never said it before, I never even wanted to, but if I said it now I'd mean it more than anything I've ever meant."

"Say it."

"I'll whisper it."

"No, say it. Say it."

"I'll say it somewhere else."

"Say it here. Say it now."

"And then we'll go out."

"Yes, we'll go out."

"Ann, I love you."

"Oh, Robert." Her arms went around his neck. "Robert, that's——"

"Let's go."

"If you say it again!"

"I said it already."

"Only if you say it again!"

"Do you enjoy it? Does it make you happy? Do you want me on my hands and knees groveling around? Are you trying to hurt me? Would you like to hurt me? You can't hurt me any more."

"I don't want to hurt you. Please, please."

"Please, what?"

She closed her eyes. "Say it."

"Ann. My Ann. Why are you like this? How can you be like this? Are you praying to me? What are you doing? Are you through trying to hurt me?"

"Robert, you'll make me cry."

"Don't cry, Ann. I love you."

"At last!" Debbie said. "Now why don't you vamoose—both of you?"

"Thank God," I said. "He came through!"

"I always come through," Robert said. He brought Ann to her feet. "I can make anybody!" He drew her close to him. "Can't I?"

"But don't," she whispered.

Robert put his arm around her waist, and they staggered out, clutching to each other. We could hear them laugh a little in the corridor.

"Wonder what they're doing?" Debbie asked, solemn again.

"Who knows? And why should we care?"

She hiccoughed. "She didn't look well. She didn't look well at all." She got to her feet, and then for a few seconds she didn't seem to know where she was. I bobbed up, and felt like I had left my whole weight behind on the sofa; it came back to me with a booming sound. We clung to each other. I was sweating. The room was racing clockwise, then in the other direction, more slowly; then it stood still.

She disengaged. "I'm all right now. Let me go to her."

"Why?"

"She's my best friend and she didn't look well, that's why."

I knew what I was doing with an instinct that told me to be sharper than she was. "They don't want you to follow. Robert will just get mad."

Tears stuck in her eyes. "It's my fault. It's all my fault!"

"Dear Debbie! Nothing's your fault."

"I chased her away."

"He took her away. It wasn't you. Now be a happy little Debbie."

"Don't call me little! Oh, this is terrible," she wailed. "It's just terrible!"

"No. It's tremendous. We're alone. Isn't that tremendous?"

"I'm her friend, I've known her all these years, I've loved her family, I've loved her; and now she's gone and I let her go to that . . . !"

"Debbie, we're all friends, but you can't follow her. Some places friends just don't. Now be happy! Our friends are in love with each other. And we're in love with each other!" Then I knew I was high, still not really high, it was not like the night I got drunk and wrote Kathy the letter.

She stared at me with the brows arched over her vivid gray eyes. "Are you in love with me?"

"Oh, God, yes—I'm crazy about you!" And I meant it, and it was true.

She smiled calmly and went over to the bar. I made us another drink of whisky, vodka, gin, and soda. She leaned her elbows on the black glass counter, looked at what I was doing, and raised her eyebrows again. I shrugged. She stared up at me from the level of my shoulder. "Why do you love me?"

"You're tremendous!"

"Ha, ha, ha." She moved down the counter, glanced at herself in the mirror opposite and smoothed the sides of her black hair. She seemed to be drawing into herself. "I'm terrible. When I think about Ann . . ."

"Forget about Ann!"

She stared down at the drink I was handing her. "What a bartender you'd make."

"All I'd like to make——"

"—is me."

I smiled.

"Oh, I bet you would! Like your friend—I hate him—that creep—it's all you're interested in."

"No, it isn't!"

"Oh, it is so! You and your *friend* in there . . . While I'm doing nothing to stop it but standing here, talking to you, trying to get you away from me!"

"Are you trying to get me away from you?"

She gave me a searching look. "What do you think I am? Do you think I approve of what she's doing?"

"No," I said, "you're tremendous, you don't think bad things."

She came into my arms suddenly. "You don't think them either, do you?"

"I told you I'm a horrible character."

"Oh." We kissed again, lingeringly. But then she broke away with strong hands. She laughed. "For a moment there," she said cruelly, "I thought I'd have to be careful. I thought I had something to be afraid of, that I'd have to keep my guard up against you!"

"Goddamn it!" I said.

"Showing your true colors, aren't you?"

"Goddamn my true colors! Goddamn your eyes, damn your mouth, damn your breasts!"

She hit me.

She was too pretty to hit back. I moved away from her, holding onto the counter, then turned, so I was facing away from her. The room was jumping, I saw flashes in front of my eyes; I knew who it was behind me. I didn't have to look to know who it was behind me. She took a step when I took a step, she stopped when I stopped, she breathed when I breathed, she had never been away from me— I had never been near her. I loved her, but she did not love me. I cried for her, but she did not cry for me.

"Jack!"

I was on the sofa. I felt her hands touch my shoulders.

"Jack," she said. "Jack, poor darling. Oh, now, Jack!"

I raised myself a little. My tears tickled my nose.

"Jack, sweetheart," she said.

"Debbie, I never should have said those things."

"Jack," she said, "look at you." She smiled. "I'm to blame."

Who was she caressing? I thought. Who was she making love to? Who was she showing tenderness for? We were nothing but what we had been taught to feel, we played in the vacant places we could never fill in each other's heart.

She raised me further, and kissed me softly on the mouth. I made hers wet with my tears. I was ashamed of my tears. "You're kind to me. I'm pathetic. I don't deserve you, do I?"

"Don't ever say that."

"I love you."

She shuddered. "I love you, Jack."

I began to tremble a little. "Love. Love. You make me so happy, love."

"You make me happy, too. Very . . . much."

I looked into her eyes, they were my eyes, they belonged to me. She belonged to me. I reached my hand up to her blouse, undid the first button; I saw the curve of her breasts, the warm, smooth thrust of her breasts, and it seemed magic that something so beautiful could lie hidden there. My hand trembled so much I could not undo the second button. She undid it for me, and her long, delicate fingers moved to the third, and then she unhooked her bra for me, too.

She smiled a beautiful giving smile. I started to take the bra away, she hesitated, then let me. I kissed her small white breasts and felt them grow firm.

"I'll make you happy," I said in a minute. "I'll always try to make you happy." The drinks had taken away whatever embarrassment we would have felt.

"I'll try to make you happy, too. We'll love each other and we'll be so happy together, won't we?"

"God, yes."

"But that's a long time from *now,*" she said.

"Yes, but it doesn't matter."

"Maybe it does matter . . ." She started ticklishly and laughed.

My hand froze. I looked into her amused eyes and no longer knew who she was, but whoever she was, she no longer belonged to me. I suddenly knew I wasn't the first, but all my thinking had been directed as if I had been the first. As I drew back, she buttoned her blouse. She looked so sad suddenly, so dejected, and ashamed, tears came into my eyes. I knew it was my fault. My head was swimming.

She did not speak.

"You're so very wonderful," I said, "I'm glad—that we met."

"Are you disgusted with me?" she asked coldly.

"No."

She did not say anything.

I put my arm around her shoulders woodenly. She was rigid. "I'll make you another drink."

"Do something."

I got up. I grew dizzy, and my legs felt like water. But I

cleared my head and made her another drink. "Thanks."

"How do you feel?" I asked.

She would not answer. "What happened to us?"

"I don't know."

"You flattered yourself *so* much. Did you think you were the only boy I ever met?"

"No, I didn't think so. I was loaded."

"You cried. I had to go to you when you cried!"

"Yes, it's very embarrassing."

"Yes, it would be."

"I was drunk, of course."

"Of course!" she said.

"Didn't I ask you to marry me?"

"That was sweet," she murmured.

"It was sweet of you to say yes."

"I won't hold you to it," she laughed.

"Will you be my girl?"

"Yes, I'll be your girl."

"My secret girl I'll never even talk to?"

She sipped her drink. "You're trying to shame me."

"No, I'm not."

"Yes, you are. You want to go steady. But what have you ever done? What have you ever done for me but put a drink in my hand?"

"Nothing. Give me a chance!"

"You have your chance. Tonight was a mistake. Tonight was putting the last thing in front of the first thing. You have to start from the beginning."

I caught a glimpse of the girl I had danced with months ago at Chi-ro, not merging with me, standing apart as if to belong to no one, to exist for everybody in the room. The great actress.

"Goddamn starting from the beginning! We go together or we don't. I don't know no other way."

"Very demanding, aren't you, all of a sudden? What about all those things you said? You were such a horrible character, and you were so understanding of Ann and your buddy in the other room. Why aren't you that understanding now?"

"You can go to hell."

"What?"

"I said, go to hell."

She looked at me calmly; she seemed very pale. Her eyelashes flickered. She was hurt, and I did not know what to do. She looked down at the floor, she did not say anything.

I got up, walked around. I wasn't drunk any more. I wished to break the deadlock; I wished I knew what to say, how to feel. I did not understand why we weren't speaking to each other. I did not understand it for my life. I let myself be cruel, I felt terrific frustration, I felt I was punishing her, I felt I was dooming myself. But I could do nothing. I wanted to run to her, but I couldn't. I was glad, I was tormented. She glanced at me, I turned aside coldly. I felt ready to cry or to shout. Sweat ran over me.

Robert came out of the corridor. There was a cigarette in his mouth, and his hair was wet as if he had just combed it. My hair was still tousled; I did not understand why they always tousled your hair. His eyes were burning. He looked at us as if he were guarding some secret.

"Have you been very merry in my absence?" he asked.

We said nothing.

"The hysterics," he said, as if to explain why he was here.

"I think we'd better go now, Jack, unless you've got some unfinished business, in which case I'll wait for you out in the street."

"What are you talking about?"

He smiled, looked at Debbie, and said nothing.

"Tell me!" I said.

"The weeping of many tears. I think we'd better get out of here."

"What have you done?" Debbie cried.

"Of course, you wouldn't know. C'mon, Jack."

"I'm drunk," I said.

"You've also had it. Let's flee."

"I ought to tear your eyes out!" Debbie said.

"No, you won't," he answered. "I'll knock you down first!"

"You filthy little bastard!"

"How true that is." He smiled and lifted his hands. "The hideousness of it. I held her, I took her, and now there's hysterics, I hate the hysterics. Of course, I must admit I've never seen hysterics before."

She came toward him, lowered her head, and then started toward the other part of the house. He grabbed her arm. "When you get her calmed down—I'm sure you know how to get her calmed down—tell her I meant all those things, tell her I said good-by, only she didn't hear me, tell her I said I loved her, tell her that I love her, I love her, say I love her."

"I'll tell her nothing!"

"You'll tell her what I say!"

She hit him, cutting the corner of his mouth. He panted, stared at her.

"You chicken son-of-a-bitch!" she said.

"So you found out I really don't hit girls. Good for you."

"You're bleeding!" she said in triumph.

"I'm not the only one who bleeds tonight."

"You——" But she burst into tears.

I saw her breaking away from me before we could make up, before I had stopped being cruel, before I had said I was sorry! "Debbie!" I shouted.

She ran down the corridor, disappeared behind a door. I heard the lock click.

Robert was trembling as he grabbed my shoulders. "Tell me what you think we should do, Jack. Tell me what to do."

"Get out of here. We better get out of here."

"All right, but I'm going to see her again tomorrow. I gotta see Ann tomorrow." There were tears in his eyes. "You should have seen her in there. It wasn't funny a bit. And there wasn't nuthin' I could do. I never should've been born, do you know that? If I had never been born, then I wouldn't have hurt her."

We went outside. It was cold, very clear, and you could see every star. We breathed frost. I felt I was walking in a nightmare.

11

I had strange dreams that night, and always at the end of them, my arm was around the waist of a girl whose face I could not see, and I was very happy. When I woke up, the memory of my happiness seemed almost as important and vivid as our party last night.

At school I found Robert in good spirits, too, even though his father's "blood vessels were bursting" because he had come home so late.

"He said he was going to beat my permission to go to New York if I wasn't *good.*"

It was hardly news.

"You're not going to try to see Ann today, are you?"

"Of course. Naturally. I'm throwing my handsomeness at her as she faints."

"You think she'll faint, do you?"

"Of course. You don't seem to realize how tremendous I am. The ermine drapes as I walk in—the prince."

"Don't tell me you're just going to walk up to her house?"

"No. She won't be there anyway. Dad will be raising his shotgun—and a thousand expeditions to Mexico to marry.

No. Slightly. I'll phone from Westwood, and she can rush over."

"I gotta go to the dentist."

"All right! She won't be home from the beach till around six, anyway."

"She wasn't much in the mood to see you last night," I said.

"Don't throw hysterics and tantrums and weeping as you run around arguing against everything! She's had time to think it over, lying around on the beach—with the beer can in her hand. And she's waiting happily."

We reached the dentist's office around four. His name was Holt, and this made Robert think of cowboys. I asked him please, not to cause any trouble.

It was a residential neighborhood, and one did not make much noise in such a place. We climbed the outside staircase of the duplex medical building and found the door locked with a note stuck on the knocker.

The doctor was resting and could not be disturbed.

"Oh, Tim!" Robert shouted into the mail slot. "Get out the six-shooter! Ride 'em, cowboy! The posse is waiting!"

Someone shouted obscenely inside.

"Oh, Tim," Robert said, "the sheriff is waiting! Get your gang and c'mon!"

I was petrified. But when I heard somebody storming toward the door, I ran downstairs like crazy, laughing but still afraid. Robert ducked into the ground floor entrance; I hesitated, my heart pounding, then followed. He wasn't in the main corridor, nor by the staircase either. But hearing a creaking, metallic sound, I whirled. He rushed toward me in a utility wheel chair.

I pushed him into the elevator and, alone, we rode up to the second story; he rolled down the corridor to Doctor Holt's door, screamed, and then rolled back into the elevator. As we shot down, I could hear the door bang open.

"I'm gonna pull a brodie," he said, and as the doors opened, sped out into the hallway, braked the wheels with a screech and looked back at the skid marks he had traced over the floor.

An anonymous door opened, and a nurse peered out.

"Leave a cripple be," he said.

The door closed reverently.

"Let's send it on a ride," I said, "before they get wise."

He stood up; I opened the glass door; he whipped it out. It passed within inches of me, hit the downhill sidewalk going like a ball of fire, bounced a little ways, lurched, and took a nose dive into the gutter. We ran with a passion.

After a fast ride to the Sunset Coffee Shop in Westwood, we had a couple of hours to kill. Over coffee we gave each other special names. I was "JaClarApTan"—the first two syllables standing for my true name abbreviated, the third for Apollo, one of the king gods, and the last because I was always supposed to be throwing tantrums. Robert was "RobGarMerCom"—"Mer" for Mercury, because of his speed with girls, and "Com" because of his many complexes. We also gave ourselves royal aliases for pick-ups, "Earl" and "Duke" and "Count."

Three UCLA girls came in and sat down in a booth in back. Robert followed them over, and I followed Robert. We were bored with waiting.

"Oh, I see the seat isn't taken," he said, and dropped down on the far side of the booth.

The girl in the middle was a blonde, the other two were brownettes. The latter seemed to be sisters; they had moles on their faces, thick, unprettified brows, and dark, intent eyes. The blonde had pretty, sculptured features and quick blue eyes; she was wearing a jumper and a red-check blouse.

I did not know why we were here, but I got a feeling that Robert wanted to prove himself, to undercut the "coms" by matching wits successfully with a trio from UCLA.

"How are you?" he asked. "The name is Earl."

"I'm Duke," I said, not even wincing.

"He's from Europe," Robert explained. "He speaks little English."

Only the blonde was amused. She wore several thin gold bracelets, and when she moved, they would slide back and jangle together. I thought when I had a girl I would like to give her bracelets like those.

"I love these original ones," one of the sisters said coldly.

"Yes, all the girls love the Prince John touch. You may leave now. A thousand unwelcomes to you."

"Where do you go to school?" the blonde asked.

"At the college." He leaned forward quickly. "Let me see your wallet."

She gave it to us, and we pored over the pictures in the folders.

"Can I see your wallet now?" he asked the sister he did not welcome.

"Nothing in there would interest you."

"I realize you have no friends, but you can give it to me anyway."

She threw it down on the table.

Robert, flipping through the folder, paused over a picture of a fat man. "Who's the elephant?"

"That's my father," she sputtered, snatching it away. "Let's ignore them," she told the girls, "maybe they'll take the hint."

"Later!" Robert said. "I'm sure they obey the unwanted one with the father waving his trunk."

The blonde laughed.

"Isn't the unwanted one hilarious?" Robert demanded. "She thinks she's a queen, and her plans have to be obeyed. She stays up at night thinking about how to become powerful, and she tries to beat everybody, she runs around screaming 'I'm the queen!' "

Both sisters laughed.

"Queen Emily," the other sister said.

"Emily!" Robert responded. "When's the tiger hunt?"

"What tiger hunt?" the blonde asked.

"You know, where you use the elephants?"

Emily gripped her hand around a glass of water menacingly.

"Save the water for Daddy. When he takes a bath, he needs so much water."

"He's kidding," I said. "He always thinks in terms of animals."

"So—I'll be over to your house around eight," he told the blonde.

"You will, will you?"

"In the El Dorado. I'm leaving now, I have to make some phone calls. I have to cancel all my other dates. Good-by!"

"Good riddance," Emily said, staring at her glass of water.

"Don't worry," he was sliding out of the booth, "I don't have a hunting license. Daddy's safe."

She threw the water. It fell short. People stood up.

"You should take it easy sometime," he said.

"What have I done!" she cried. "How stupid that was!"

"Oh, you don't have to admit your faults. They're so obvious."

We moved to the phone booths in back.

"Did you have to treat her like that?" I asked.

"I don't know what got into me." He went into an empty phone booth. "Things like that are always getting into me, though. I guess I don't really like girls very much except when I can run around with them." He lifted the receiver. "You might as well come in here with me. Then if I am to be beaten, you can shout slogans and Ann will cry, 'Oh, I'm crushed.' And the tears will electrocute us."

After he shut the door to the booth, I could hardly move. I lit a cigarette and as he dialed, he lit one, too.

"Hello?" said a young man's voice on the other end.

I could hear plainly.

"Hello!" Robert shouted into the receiver. "Where's Ann?"

"Do you wish to talk to Ann?"

"Yeah."

"She ain't here."

"Who is this?"

"Her brother."

"Oh, it is, huh? Where did Ann go?"

"Who wants to know?"

"Her boy friend," Robert said.

"I know her boy friend's voice well enough to know you ain't him."

"Where did she go?"

"She told me somebody's been bothering her, and I got a notion you're the one. What's your name, anyway?"

"Robert."

"You're the one."

"The hell I'm the one. What do you know about it, you punk?"

"Just you hold on a minute, buster."

There was a silence and then an older man's voice said, "Look, son, I think you're wasting your time."

"I'm wasting my time, am I? Who are you?"

"Ann's father."

"Oh. Of course, I'm anxious to meet you."

"Look, son, I don't know who you are, but I think you ought to get this straight, you're wasting your time."

"You already said that."

"Maybe it bears repeating."

"Oh, get out."

It was getting very warm in the booth.

"What did you say?"

His voice cracked. "I said, get out! Back to your wife and the apron strings!"

He hung up and dialed another number immediately. My eyes were smarting with our cigarette smoke, but he wouldn't let me open the door, and I couldn't open it by myself because of the way we were standing.

"Hello?" a voice said on the other end.

"Hello, Mac, is that you? It's me, Robert."

"Hi."

"Hi!" I shouted from the background. Sweat was rolling off my forehead; cigarette smoke seemed to persist in my nostrils.

"You having a party or something?" Mac asked.

"Yes, we're all gathered in the phone booth. Listen! Your pal, Ann's boy friend—the cat—I gotta get hold of him. A thousand debts to be owed as you give me his number."

A silence. Then—"What's it about?"

"I want some information from him about a certain guy who's been cutting in on my girl."

"Maybe I can help you."

"Oh, beat off, will you? Beat your wings and hurry to your nest and get the number."

"The number is Arizona one-nine-nine-six-seven."

"Oh, you knew it by heart, didn't you?"

"I know a lot of numbers by heart."

"But you know this one especially well, don't you, little eagle?" Robert asked.

"Little eagle?" Mac repeated.

"You knew it that night you informed, didn't you?"

Silence.

"Didn't you know it, little eagle?"

"You mean that night——"

"We know what we're talking about, don't we, unrolling stone gathering moss?" Robert was on his second cigarette. Clouds of smoke bounced against the windows of the booth.

"How can something like that bother you now?" Mac asked.

"Because it means you're a fink and a traitor."

"To you, but not to the majority of my friends."

"—your friends! You're an utter fink."

"You sound like a criminal."

"You sound like an idiot. You also look like one."

"Go to hell."

"Ladies first."

"—you!"

"Oh, would you like to? I thought you promised me you were going to die."

"I thought you promised me you'd become a complete spastic."

"I wouldn't interrupt your act. I'm laying for you. Keep away from dark alleys and keep away from the mirror—you bad bald eagle!"

He got really obscene then, and Robert hung up.

"One-nine-nine-six-seven," he repeated. He called the operator, said there had been some kind of mistake, got his dime back, and dialed Ann's boy friend.

A woman answered.

"Is Fred there?" Robert asked.

"He's out for the evening," she said melodiously. "I'm his mother. Can I take a message?"

"I'm his old buddy, I haven't seen him in eight years, maybe you could tell me where he is, and I could meet him."

"He said he was going to the Brentwood tonight."

The Brentwood was across the street from the coffee shop. We had met Kathy's sister there.

"Good, maybe I can catch him. Did he go alone?"

"Oh no."

"What does that mean?"

"He went on a date."

"Who did he go with?" he demanded.

"He—went with his steady girl friend," she answered bewilderedly.

"What's her name, maybe I know her?"

There was a short silence.

"Well—her name is Ann."

"Ann Fields?" he cried.

"Is something wrong?"

"What do you care? Is it Ann Fields?"

"Yes, it's Ann Fields. What's this all about, anyway?"

"So he went with her! So he did! So that's what happened!"

"What's *wrong* with you?"

I started to cough. My shirt was soaked. I tried to crash out the door.

"Hello," a man's voice said over the phone, "what is this, are you looking for trouble?"

"I'm looking for your son!"

"Forget it!" I said. "Let me outa here!"

"What do you want with my son?" his father demanded.

"I'm fighting him. The next you'll see of him he'll be in an ambulance!"

"I'm calling the police. They'll deal with your gang!"

"All twenty-five of us? I'm sorry! Back to the dishes, Dad!"

"It's a joke," his mother said in the background. "Tom, it's some kind of joke!"

"Hang up, I want to get out of here!" I cried.

"All right, son, it's very funny," his father said. "I just hope it doesn't rub my boy the wrong way."

"Why?"

"Because my boy has a habit of putting away characters."

"Then *I'm* calling the police."

I smashed my fists against the door. An old lady on her way to the rest room stopped and stared at me. I made horrible faces at her. Her eyes widened, her mouth parted. She had a mouth like a frog's.

"You ought to go to bed, son," Fred's father went on jovially, "you've had one too many!"

"I guess you're right," Robert said, "but before I go to bed I have to get a girl."

"A girl? Oh, is that right, my boy?"

"Yeah. And guess which girl it'll be? Your son's! I'll take her. You wait. She isn't his, she's mine!"

"Ha, ha!"

"Hah!"

He hung up.

We burst out of the booth, taking with us terrific streams of smoke.

Anxiety sprang into the old lady's eyes. "Fire!" she screamed. "Fire! Fire! Fire!"

The manager, a tall man in a brown suit, rushed up. "Where? Where?" he shouted.

"Granny was just throwing a spasm," Robert said.

The manager glared at him. "You again! Get out of here!"

"Are you throwing me out?"

"You're damn right I am!"

We marched to the door.

"Can't I come back ever?" Robert asked.

"No, you can't come back ever."

The theater wouldn't open for an hour yet, so we went to a drugstore, had hamburgers and read pocket books and magazines at the racks to kill time. Robert was tense, and I was, too. The time went by very fast.

12

We argued over our age at the box office but finally got in for juniors: I had a month to go at the cut rates and held onto my status savagely. Robert bought popcorn, and we climbed up the carpeted staircase from the foyer to the small balcony. Everyone we knew always sat upstairs.

The usher said there weren't any seats.

"I'm looking for somebody," Robert answered politely. We marched halfway down the aisle, scanning rows of darkened faces. "I see her," he whispered to me. "Now let's find some seats."

We crossed over to the mezzanine and went up the second aisle. At last he stopped in front of two small boys, and drew the attention of the closest. "What's your name?" he whispered.

"Ricky."

"You're wanted. Your mother's waiting for you down in the lobby."

"Oh, gee!"

"Shut up and get down to the lobby." He touched the shoulder of the second. "What's your name?"

"Snodgrass!" he said impudently.

"Well, get the hell down in the lobby, she's waiting for you, too."

"Who says?"

"I say. Get out!"

They scurried out of their seats and tramped up the aisle bitterly.

We replaced them. I sank down in the seat like a criminal.

"What's playing?" Robert asked me.

"I don't know, Stranger."

Somebody said, "Shh!"

He crunched on popcorn. "We mustn't disturb," he said loudly. "This is so tremendous."

Judy Holliday was nursing a baby.

"She thinks she can act," he said.

I sank lower in the seat. "Shut up."

"Why?"

A small-sized bit actor came on the screen.

"May we be short," he said.

I laughed.

The bit actor took a prat fall. The audience laughed.

"Uh!" Robert put in. "So hilarious I nearly died."

The balcony grew boisterous. Everybody was shushing each other. The usher's flashlight kept waving in our faces.

"Can't we get it a little quiet around here?" Robert demanded.

"I'll see what I can do, sir." The usher moved on down the aisle, flashing his light in other rows.

Robert kept me laughing. The more I wanted him to shut up, the harder he made me laugh. But I knew why he was so agitated tonight. He couldn't concentrate on the picture a second.

"Get outa my seat!" the little boy said at his elbow.

"Oh, you're back!" Robert said. "What do you want?"

"Gimme my seat!"

"I'll give you a kick in the pants. Now get out and find your poor mother!"

"She ain't here!"

"She said if she couldn't wait, you had to walk home immediately."

"I live nine miles away!" he answered, tears springing to his eyes.

"All right, don't cry." He stood up. "Here's your seat."

"Oh, gee!" he sobbed.

Robert put his hand on the boy's head. "I have a little boy just like you at home. I'll tell you what. Take this popcorn here." He whispered to him in a secret voice. "Also take this dime. Now dump this popcorn over the mezzanine railing and then you can spend this dime on whatever you want."

"Okay."

"Don't let anybody see you."

The two little boys stole off toward the mezzanine.

We scrambled up the stairs.

"Why did you do that?" I hissed.

"Why not?"

Suddenly he cut to his left and started to make his way into a row of seats.

"C'mon!" he said.

I didn't want to follow. But he stopped dead in his tracks, waiting for me; there was a tremendous commotion and, my temples pounding, I plunged after him.

"Pardon me, I'm sorry, pardon me," I kept saying. He

said, "Coming through, damn it, coming through. Are you all right there?"

He seemed to struggle, push, shove and fall over one particular patron. I thought all hell was going to break loose. Then I recognized her; it was Ann. She looked amazed, petrified.

He broke past her and pushed into Fred.

"Move it," the older boy said.

"You look like an idiot," Robert answered.

Fred leapt up, they both plunged forward, and then they were locked together, their heads down like a pair of bulls, swaying back and forth. Fred shoved him backward, past Ann. Everyone stood up, and I had to push my way out to the aisle.

"Get him!" someone shouted.

The usher raced down the steps, cut past me, and struggled through the throng.

Screams and shouts came from the orchestra. I guessed it was the popcorn drifting over their heads.

Robert fell back and went down. I could see him try to get up. Fred was flailing with his fists.

They grunted, and I could seem to perceive the sharp smell of sweat from their bodies.

"Jack!"

Seeing the usher wasn't going to get through on my side for a few minutes at least, I ran down to the mezzanine, crossed over, and rushed up the second staircase. I was much nearer to him now. I could hear them gasping. I kept imagining all those feet near his head—the heavy brogue shoes of some of Fred's friends. I leaped up on the row of seats behind which they were struggling, teetered, balanced past the standing patrons; one seat gave way, trapping my foot for a few seconds. But finally I reached the place where they lay. Sprawling over the seat rim, I grabbed hold of Fred's jacket. He didn't budge. He had inched up on Robert until his chest was smothering his face. I could hear loud gasps and knew he was pressing down hard; I let go of the jacket and clutched his hair.

He still didn't move.

My legs were shaking like a leaf. I put all my strength into my arm and lifted. Then Fred gave way with a cry. I kept lifting him by the hair. He rose to his knees, bent back, and struck out at me with his open hand. I took it on the side of my face, and didn't let go. Then he hit me again, and I did let go.

Robert leaped over the row I was in. The usher grabbed for him, missed, doubled up on the back of the seat. We scrambled over to the staircase, and took the steps in two seconds flat.

Robert's face was flaming red, his hair stuck out like a wild man's, his shirt was wrinkled as if he'd slept in it. We raced down the stairs to the lobby. The manager was standing by the door.

"Hey, you two!" he said.

We ducked into a side aisle of the theater, and where the curtain, marking the loges, and a bend in the width of the tapering rows hid us from view of the lobby, I collapsed into a seat next to a girl. The two of us would have been obvious, and Robert kept running.

I threw my arm around the rim of the girl's seat and smiled at her through heavy panting and what felt like a slight slavering at the mouth.

She glanced over impudently. "Why don't you take a picture?"

I figured she was about thirteen. But I had never figured out an answer for 'Why don't you take a picture.'

The manager went past me in a fast walk, and I spotted Robert hotfooting it way down in front. Usherettes, posted at the head of all the aisles, switched on their flashlights and began marching down methodically, like cops closing in.

Robert started to cut over to the other side, but at the halfway point, I lost him. I figured he was on the far aisle, all right, but I was afraid they would find him. I tried to lose myself in Judy Holliday and couldn't; my legs trembled, and my hand on the rim of the seat began to tingle.

Then I got a hope. If we could hold out till the intermission, they'd never find us. I thought of making a break for one of the exits, but I had never been able to open one in less than five minutes—anyway, afterward I wouldn't know where Robert was. The manager was directing the search, and he concentrated on the points where he had seen Robert last. I figured Robert was safe from him at least, but I caught sight of the usherette on the far side proceeding down front with her flashlight. A minute later the light was off. I saw her going up the aisle alone.

The picture ended, they played Gilbert and Sullivan, asking you to find the treasure at the refreshment bar, all the lights went on, and it was intermission. I passed into the lobby with the crowd, cut over to the far aisle, and watched everybody coming out.

"Can I help you?" the usherette asked.

"I—" I stopped. It was the pretty blonde we had talked to in the Sunset two hours ago.

She raised her eyebrows, and her eyes smiled quickly in recognition.

"Where is he?" I whispered.

"He's outside by now. He said he'd wait for you across the street."

"You found him?"

"Sure." She smiled. "There he was, with the most sorry look on his face. He looked very far from having an El Dorado just then."

"What's your name?"

"Sue."

"Sue, you're a dream."

"You little boys, when are you ever going to grow up?"

"We're grown-up," I said.

She smiled.

"Good-by," I said.

I crossed the lobby. The manager was standing watchfully by the door. A small crowd was under the marquee smoking. I lit a cigarette and stepped outside. I saw Robert standing on the corner across the street. He waved to me, and I joined him.

"You really had luck going for you," I said.

He scowled.

"What's the matter?"

"Let's get outa here."

"Where will we go?"

"Your house. I want to sleep over at your house tonight. Do you mind?"

"No."

We started walking down to Wilshire. "I'm going to see Ann tomorrow," he said.

"My God, again?"

"Yes, again! I'll figure out a way. I'll meet her someplace."

"I'm sorry you lost the fight."

"So am I. Thanks for pulling his hair."

"I suppose you've got it all planned how you can destroy him mentally?"

"You mean by telling him what I did to his girl?" He shoved his hands deeper in his pockets. "I'm not going to tell him nothing. Because you know what would happen? He'd forgive her! The filthy hun."

"What's wrong with forgiving?"

"He'd demand what I got, and he'd get it, you can believe me!"

"All right; why don't we leave them alone?"

"I'd like to, but I can't, I'd like to forget her and forget everything and forget this stupid Westwood Village, but I can't! Just like I can't forget I'm nothing, I'm unknown, I'm something they did together in a room one night."

I wanted to help. "I know you believe it, but you've never convinced me. I'm your best friend, so I should be easy to convince."

"I never been handed a piece of paper that says, 'You're s——' I don't need no piece of paper. Some things you know without nobody telling you."

"I'm not sure about that."

"Listen, when you were little did you ever wonder—if you were all right? Did you ever go to your mother and say, 'Did I really come from you? Or did you just find me?' "

"I suppose I did."

"Everybody does! But I never asked because I was afraid of what they might tell me."

"There you are!"

"There you are in a barrel of crap! I ain't the smartest guy that ever walked the earth—the dictionary isn't memorized yet—but I've always been afraid, ever since I was little *I wanted to know!*"

"And you don't know," I said.

"Why do you think I want to go to New York? *Because* I don't know!"

"All right, forget it. But couldn't you take for granted your father is your real father for the time being?"

"I've been taking it for granted for years."

"All right," I said, "I'm sorry, let's drop it completely."

We arrived late at my house. He couldn't seem to bring himself to undress even when I was already in bed. I sat up reading a book. My bed was against the wall, and I could look straight ahead to the windows. There were two bureaus against the north and south walls and a desk under the window littered with papers and a school book I never read.

"What's the matter with you?" I asked finally.

He crossed the room and looked out the window into the night. "I can't sleep. I can't lose myself. I don't want to forget what's happening every minute."

"You're being a maniac again."

He stared out of the window.

"What're you looking at?"

"I don't know. It's so peaceful out there. You know what I mean?" He leaned forward on the sill. "Nobody's doin' nuthin' . . ."

"Yes, they are. Only you can't see them."

"Remember us? Last night?"

"I remember."

He grew silent. It was very still. I continued reading an old copy of Mickey Spillane.

"I can see the taillights of a plane," he said. "You ever got the feeling you'd just like to get on a plane and ride out in the night?"

"Hell, no."

"I mean just go, and not come back, and not have to think about coming back, and look down on all the people, and all the peaceful nights that they can see if they're awake."

"You want to die, for crying out loud?"

He looked around at me suddenly. "No, I don't want to die. Is that really what it sounds like to you?"

"If you go to bed, maybe I'd change my mind about it."

"I'm not going to bed."

"Well, that's dandy. Couldn't you have done this at home?"

"Oh, you can go to sleep if you want."

"Can I really go to sleep?"

"Oh, quit throwing spasms. I won't bother you. Later on I'll try to go to sleep, too."

I turned off the light, but I couldn't sleep with him prowling around the room. Later when he thought I was dead to the world, he switched the desk lamp on and picked up something to read. Unspeakable rage churned in me. I waited for a few minutes, then reared up, flinging away my blanket, sprang out of bed, and half roared an obscenity. He started and dropped the book, and I was revenged.

"You're a merry little soul," he said after a few seconds. "What're you looking for, your pipe?"

"Damn you! I won't be able to sleep for hours! Thanks! Thanks a lot!"

He growled like a dog. "Down." Then he picked up the book and sprawled out on the cot.

It was then I spied the school books he had left with me this afternoon. Normally I did not pry. I had always felt like it, though, the marked tests and the homework of somebody else always made me curious. When he noticed what I was doing, it was too late to tell me to stop.

I did not find much to interest me. What I was mainly after were the compositions, so I could have something to ride him about— I was not so hot in mathematics either. Toward the end I found the only composition. It was graded C and there was a note—"See me after class."

I read:

How I Spent My Vacation in 1,000 Words

by Robert Garrety, Esq.

Dear Father Kelly (S.J.), since I have never been off vacation—since I am always loafing and would like to ride rods all day and do nothing, well, since that is the case, writing about my vacation would be to write you the story of my life. Since that would take too long, I will write about a dream I had.

I have this dream, well, it is a nightmare. I'm running in the streets of New York, and I reach my mother's apartment house and start to climb the steps. There're hundreds of steps, and when I reach the top, I'm worn out, I'm exhausted. I practically crawl over to her door, I can hardly keep my eyes open. Then through the door my mother tells me to come in. But I can't open the door, I can't move! She says, 'Hurry, Robert!' but I can't— I can't do anything! Then she says, my mother—she says, 'Hurry, hurry, Robert,' and I still can't do anything. Then she doesn't say anything, and I know she's gone.

There's another part to the dream—I'm going down the steps again. Then I see this hideous man coming up. His face is all bloody. I try to run, but I can't; I can't move at all any more. And he keeps coming, he keeps coming!

That is my dream. I see it does not quite run to 1,000 words. It took me three hours to write.

It made me afraid just reading it. He got up and looked over my shoulder.

"I forgot that was in there," he said. He grabbed the binder.

"What did the teacher say to you after class?"

"Nothing. I don't know why I wrote it. I'm sure I'm going to write a thousand words about my vacation."

"Maybe you wrote it because he's a priest."

"Why? What's so shocking about it?"

"I don't know. But it's shocking."

He sat down beside me. "What do you think about it?"

I looked at the composition again. "Who's the hideous man supposed to be?"

"I don't know, some monster."

"Why do you say 'He kept coming' twice?"

"Because that's what he did, he kept comin'."

"You know what we mean when we say it."

"That isn't what I meant."

"How do you know?"

He thought a minute. "He was just some monster."

"Who do you think your real father is?"

He got up, dropped his binder on the cot, and then went to the window. "I guess I do think he's kind of a monster, my real father. I don't want to think that. I don't want to do that to myself. Sometimes, I know, I stink." He took a deep breath, exhaled rapidly. "She has to tell me about him.

My mother has to tell me who he was and what he was like. Oh, God, but I wish untrue father was my real father." He turned back and scowling like he was about to collapse, he leaned against the sill. "I like untrue father; I wish he was my real father. I remember one time when my mother was visiting three years ago, I did something and untrue father stopped me and my mother didn't like that, and she said, 'Robert, you have more me in you than him,' and untrue father, he looked very sad. And then he looked angry and there was a fight, and I ran out of the room."

"Why didn't you ask your mother about it then?"

"I did ask her. I was eleven. Do you think she got serious with me? No, sorry. After a while I didn't know what to say any more."

"Once you asked me to write her a letter. I could still do it for you."

"I was stupid then. I was thinking too much about her. Since I have Ann I don't think so much about my mother any more."

"But I could write the letter."

He came back to the cot, and sprawled out. "You're stupid if you think she'd actually tell me. I have to force it out of her, or beg her— I don't know. You never know how you're going to be with a dame till you're with her."

"With your own mother?"

"My mother's a woman. I love her and that doesn't matter. She loves me and that won't matter. She's not going to throw the information at me. Do you think that's something she'd like to tell?"

"I guess not."

"But I'll have her tell me. We'll talk about it, and then I'll know and I'll be . . . changed."

"You think you'll be changed?"

"Won't that be enough to change me?" He rolled over on his stomach and looked at me. "Do you want to talk about when you're married?"

I shook my head. "I never think about it . . ."

"That's all girls think about. I know it's hideous so I'm going to have a mistress."

"Who?"

"Guess who!"

"I can't."

"Oh, go to hell." He rolled over on his back again. "She'll love me—don't laugh, it means free sex, you know. And we'll all be happy, and I'll run around spending money, and we'll go to the beach at night. Ann won't be the hysterical type by that time, and we'll rent a thousand motels. And I'll tell her the story of my life, and she'll love me—and I'll say, 'I love you'—don't laugh, Jack—'because you're a thousand ages above me and I look at you and I want to be good'—don't laugh at this part—'and I love you'—I said 'I love you,' didn't I? Well, you know, I'll say it a lot. They like you to say it. They're stupid. And I'll tell her, 'You can understand me, you make me happy. Oh, you make me happy.' That'll kill her, won't it? And then I'll say, I'll say, 'You're closest to me of everybody that's ever been closest to me, even my friend JaClarApTan, and even my mother, and my father, and my untrue father, and steppy who thinks she's a mother, because I love you best.' So. That's the way it is. Are you croaking from laughter?"

"I didn't see anything to laugh at."

He turned over, looked at me with his burning cat's eyes. "Then you're stupid," he said.

I didn't say anything. He grew silent. I read a little, then turned off the light, and went to sleep. For a while I was conscious of him on the rim of sleep, and then, imperceptibly, I lost all track.

13

I woke up with the alarm clock, which I had forgotten to turn off, and lay still a moment swearing to myself. Then I sat up suddenly, leaned over, and silenced it. The room was chilly; bars of congealed sunlight lay on the floor; outside was the roaring of traffic from the boulevards. Robert was sitting in a chair facing me, his head leaning against the wing. I looked at him, his eyes opened, and he stared back.

"I had a dream," he said softly.

I grunted with the unnatural voice of awakening. He talked as if he had never been to sleep, and he talked to me out of the influence of his dream.

"I met Ann for the first time again . . . It was a very happy thing. It was in technicolor—it was all very merry."

"Good."

Suddenly he frowned, got to his feet, and staggered over to the window. "I feel happy. It's going to be warm today. Look at the sky."

"Look at it for me."

"Oh, what a sky!"

"What is it like?"

"It's blue, real blue, there ain't no clouds, and the sun's just come up."

"From the way you were talking I thought it had turned green or something. Good night, I mean, good-by. Hell! I'm going back to sleep." I buried my head in the pillow.

"You've been asleep! Look at me, I'm up!"

"All right, all right!" I said. I got out of bed. I didn't know what I was doing. I had some idea I had to obey people who told me to get out of bed; it was a school-day habit that carried over to the weekend holidays.

"We'll eat breakfast right away," he said, "and then we'll head up to Westwood."

I got dressed bitterly. He threw water on his face and combed his hair. He was very pale-looking, and his eyes seemed a little dull.

"How much sleep did you get last night?" I asked.

"I dozed off some. I had the light on, didn't I bother you?"

"No," I said, "you didn't. Ha, ha."

"Well," he answered, "that was my purpose, I didn't want to bother you."

"You didn't succeed very well, did you?"

"Sorry!"

We went down to the kitchen. He had three cups of coffee and ate lightly. I had a big breakfast, but I was so sleepy I kept forgetting to eat in the midst of eating it. When we walked outside, though, in the morning chill, I became more alert.

"Where do you think I should meet her?" he asked.

"Have no idea."

"If they'll let me in, I think the Sunset is about the best place. What do you think?"

"Don't know."

"Quit brooding, will you?"

"I just don't think it'll turn out all right."

"I really care what you think. But have you forgotten Debbie?"

"No."

"Don't you want to hear about her from Ann?"

"Yeah."

"Then you'll come with me?"

"Sure."

"We ought not to split up now."

"No, damn it!"

We shook hands. I thought of Kathy. I gave her Debbie's face, Debbie's words, and the things she had given me that I had never known before when I was in love. It was like a dream and the two girls were one, as they had been that night.

When we reached Westwood, it was still early. We went into a drugstore and had more coffee, read magazines at the counter, and then wandered up toward the Sunset. Robert was feeling his lack of sleep by now, despite the coffee, and he asked what he ought to do. I said we should get energy.

"How?"

"We could drink milk."

We went into a grocery store and bought two quart cartons of milk, then staggered up the sidewalk, drinking it in public like a couple of drunks. We called it "en" for energy, but never quite finished it off. They were making a movie up at UCLA. We went up there and stood in a breakfast line for free coffee, and then went down to the Sunset.

He insisted on sitting in the same booth where we had

first seen Ann. While we waited "until twenty minutes to ten, the best time to call," I began to reflect on all the horrible things that had happened to us so far.

"I don't think anything very nice is going to happen when you shout at her to come over," I said. "And don't drag Debbie into it. When I want to do something about Debbie I'll do it. All this waiting—all this stirring up more trouble . . . Hell."

He put down the newspaper he had been glancing at, folded his hands, and looked at me impassively. "Do you think I'm going to sit around another three months until I get another chance at her? I've sat around." He swallowed. "I've sat around three years waiting to see my mother. Oh, may we wait until people send us places, or people decide to see us—in New York or in Vista Canyon? May we do that? . . . doing that . . . doing that any more."

I kept looking at the restaurant clock. Finally I said: "It's a quarter to ten."

He nodded. "Do you want to come in the booth with me?"

"Not this time."

"Well, go back with me anyway. I don't want her hanging up and I'm standing there and nobody's around."

"Uh-huh."

"Remember if it goes lousy, I hate her."

"All right."

"Think up hideous things about her and start saying them as I come out the door."

"All right, all right," I said.

"But if it goes good, don't say anything, don't speak."

"You have your ways, don't you?" I said.

"Princely ways," he said.

I could hear his voice through the glass door. He dialed

and waited, shrugged at me from inside. Then he suddenly looked down at the receiver. "Hello, I'd like to talk to Ann," he said. He raised his eyebrows. "It's me," he said.

I walked away from the booth and when I came back, he seemed to be speaking in a low voice. Then suddenly he raised it. "No, now. Now!"

I walked away again, and as I turned around for the second time, I saw him emerging from the booth. He did not say anything while we walked back to our table, and I could not read his expression.

We sat down. "Well?" I asked.

He shrugged. "I convinced her to meet me. She said she guessed that would be the best thing. So she can get rid of me, I suppose. Hah! We'll see who gets rid of who."

I wanted to leave.

"No! You can be my witness—and you can approve of all my tremendous thoughts."

Thirty minutes went by, and they threatened to throw us out. I bought a lunch. The same thing happened at eleven-thirty and I bought another lunch. But Robert couldn't eat. I was drowsy with food.

"What if she doesn't come?" I said. "What if she never comes?"

"If she isn't here by twelve-fifteen, we'll go up to her house."

I wished she would come.

He drank ice-water incessantly. Now and then he would absent himself for a minute. I could see him emerging from the little room wild-eyed, staring around for her. His hands shook. Most of the time he sat with his head buried in his arms. Whenever he heard anybody come in, he would look up, blink, and when he did not see her, bury his head again.

He splashed water on his face to try to take some of the pallor away. He couldn't read, he couldn't think, he wanted to sleep, he wanted to be alert; he seemed to be living on a high wire, balancing with his nerves alone.

"It's ten after twelve," I said.

"What?" He met my eyes with his reddened ones. "Oh. So what about it?"

"The waitress is giving me the evil eye again."

"I'll pay for coffee," he said, and shot his head into the oblivion of his arms.

The coffee was cold and bitter when I thought I could safely get around to drinking it. It was twelve twenty-five. Robert was staring out the window; his eyes were very sad.

Then I heard footsteps, and looking over my shoulder, saw Ann. She hesitated outside the glass door. One hand reached out to open it, took the handle, froze. She looked at me. I tried to smile. She was wearing a red half coat, a white gold-trimmed blouse, navy wool skirt, and flats. Her face was very cherubic, flushed and healthy, her golden hair was waved; I could see the freckles sprinkled in a faint band across her nose and cheeks, and the vivid blueness of her eyes.

I turned back and looked at Robert opposite me. He was leaning forward and staring at me intelligently as if I had something to say. I leaned forward, too, and clasped my hands. We looked at each other agonizingly. Then he jerked to his feet. She glided into the booth.

"I didn't think you were ever coming," he said tremblingly.

She didn't answer for a long time. "I hardly thought I was coming, either." Her voice was low, cool.

He leaned forward as if in a spell. "I don't know what to say. It's hard to say. Except one thing. I meant it. Look at me and you can believe it." He gestured dramatically with his hand on the table, struck his glass of ice-water, and knocked it over. He was drunk with concentration and oblivious to the edges of his existence. Now he was horrified. "My God, somebody will have to clean it!"

"The waitress will clean it," I said.

"This is the horriblest thing," he said.

"Your grammar . . ." Ann's voice shook. "Your grammar." She looked as if she was disgraced.

"Does it bother you?" he demanded.

"Oh, yes, and a thousand other things bother me! What were you trying to prove last night?"

"That you're my girl."

"Your girl? Ha, ha—you think I would go steady with a freshman? And then you're so rational—always screaming and fighting; we could have been arrested last night. Fred is just furious."

"At you?"

"No, at you! He says if he ever sees you again, he'll break your neck——"

"He's a little upset, though, too, isn't he, as he roams around on his Mongolian pony, wondering what made me think I had the right to pick a fight over you."

She bit her lip, and began twisting the edges of a paper napkin.

He leaned forward. "You're mine. Ask a priest if you aren't mine."

Tears came to her eyes. "I wouldn't have you if you were the last man on earth—only you aren't a man. You wouldn't even count as a man. I'd ask a priest if you weren't going to hell, and he'd say yes. And maybe I am. But I still wouldn't have you, wouldn't even want to know you."

"I wish you would want to know me. I wish you'd bother to take the time to know me."

"I've known him a long time," I said hoarsely, "you can ask me about him."

"I can ask you about him," she said. "What do you know about anything? Just who are you? Here's a message: drop dead."

"Who's the message from?" Robert asked.

"Debbie."

"Return it as is," he said. "I wish you'd take the time to know me."

"You already said that."

"You never answered me."

"I know you as well as I'll ever want to know you."

"You don't know that I meant everything I said—that night."

"Tell me what you said."

He breathed heavily. His hands trembled. "I want to do good by you. I believe we can be happy. Very. You know."

"You can go to hell."

"Thanks."

"You're welcome." She permitted herself a smile. "That wasn't so hard! I thought you might kill me when I said that."

"I didn't, did I?"

"I thought they'd be able to hear you scream all the way to—to my house."

"I didn't scream, did I?" He seemed so relaxed he was almost dead.

"I hope—well, I hope you'll never bother me again?" she asked seriously.

"Oh no, no."

"You're all *through* with me? I hope?"

"Sure."

"I won't turn around three months from now to find you waiting. Will I?"

He shook his head, then leaned forward; it was almost as if he had fallen. "That's really what you were worried about, wasn't it?"

She searched him for a possible second meaning, then nodded brightly. "Thinking about it can give you the creeps. Wherever you go, this guy is watching you. Even if he isn't there, he's *thinking* about you. How would you like it?"

"And that's what you were worried about?"

She became more serious. "Yes."

"And the other part, the rest of it, that doesn't matter?"

"I can see you don't know *me* very well, do you? You were saying I don't know you—oh no, I should get to know you better, then—how *wonderful.*" She smiled. "Because for a minute I felt this pity . . . you're very funny. You go around threatening people and you don't mean it!"

"I don't mean it, ha, ha."

"You can't help it, it's just the way you have of expressing yourself."

"The way I have of expressing myself, ha, ha."

"I feel real good now."

"It makes you happy?" he said.

"Yes. You made it easy. It's all over with; I went through hell"—she faltered—"I was sorry, I made promises—but this was hanging over me."

"What?"

"Saying good-by."

"Say it!"

"Good-by, Robert!" She offered her hand, he took it, they shook in mock solemnity. "Good-by . . . good-by . . ."

"Yeah," he said.

"Good-by—good-by—good-by!" She softened the hold on his hand, he wrenched it back. "I'm not afraid of you any more."

"I didn't want you to be afraid of me."

She leaned forward, put her hand on his cheek. "You're cute, Robert. You'll have success—in something. I almost wish—we had been—happier."

He said nothing.

"I've got to go now," she said, picking up her purse.

"Remember me," he answered.

"I think I shall."

"Okay."

She went out.

We sat there a long time, not saying anything.

14

Robert was suspended from school the following week for drawing the face of a monster on the blackboard with a teacher's name printed under it. (He had been reprimanded by Mr. Raybourne the same day for passing notes.) He was told to write out the poem *Evangeline* three times before returning to classes, and to plan on enrolling in some other school for the fall semester—a school where he could, perhaps, find a program and teachers more suited to his taste.

Robert's father was furious about it and from then on refused even to discuss the trip to New York.

Robert did not do a thing to get Ann back; of course there was not much he could do. But if he had given up on her, her ghost had not given up on him. He had never understood her, and sometimes now when he talked to me about his mother, he sounded like he was talking about her. He seemed to transfer to his mother all of Ann's inaccessibility, all the advantage to be gained in reaching her and all the longing he had to do so.

His father had restricted him to the premises until the

Evangeline penance should be completed, but finally relented enough to suggest that he invite me over for lunch on Saturday. I didn't know the lunch was to be a special occasion, or else I wouldn't have gone, because the special occasions of other families always embarrass me.

But when I got there, there were five settings on the dining room table, a lace cloth, and a vase of new-cut roses. There was a birthday cake on the sideboard and written on it, "Happy Birthday, Daddy."

"Look," Robert said, "only twenty-five candles. Ha!"

"You didn't tell me. Maybe I should go."

"I'm afraid not. Don't worry. The ceremony is just for Paul. The real party with all the heavy drinking comes tonight. Meanwhile, we're throwing our presents at him." He reached into a cupboard and took down three gaily wrapped packages—I knew the sloppy one was his. "I did this myself."

"What is it?"

"A whip."

Just as I laughed, his mother came in from the kitchen with a big plate of sandwiches and asked him to do her a favor and call his father and Paul. When they were all collected we sat down and ate the sandwiches with milk, coffee, and water. At the end of the meal it was suggested we sing "The Happy Birthday Song." But when they came to "Happy Birthday, dear Daddy," I moved my lips silently.

"I got a letter from my mother yesterday," Robert said suddenly.

"Oh?" His father had been cutting the cake; he paused for a moment, the spatula in mid-air, then brought it down sharply, making a clean slice.

"She sent me the money to buy your present."

Mr. Garrety began putting the cake on serving plates. "This looks very good," he said. "I don't like her sending you money, Robert."

"Why?"

"I've been supporting you since you were born, and I can afford to continue doing so, that's why."

"Can't you stand it if anybody else has money? I didn't notice you giving me any money for *her* birthday gift."

"You didn't ask me."

"I didn't ask her either."

"Let's talk about this later, Robert. Finish your cake—or else leave the table."

Robert swallowed a piece of cake, sort of choked on it, then got to his feet. "Too bad one marriage wasn't good enough for you," he muttered.

"What did you say?" Mr. Garrety was on his feet, too, his chair slamming hard on the asphalt tile floor.

He caught up with Robert in the living room, pushed him onto a couch. I plunged down the hallway and tried the lock on the front door, like a dog eager to be let out. The door opened all right, but there was a latch chain restricting it; I began fumbling to unfasten it. Mr. Garrety's roar stopped me.

"You come back here and sit down, too, Jack. I don't want any one-sided versions of this getting around town."

He was too angry to oppose. I sidled back, went to a chair. He turned to Robert.

"Do you want the truth?" His blue eyes were flashing and his fists—big, hairy, freckled—were clenched at his sides. "Well, you're going to get it. I'm sorry to say it, but your mother's a tramp! It's all she is and all she ever was!"

Robert shot up. "No, she isn't!" he said in shame and fury. "You're a dirty liar!"

"Don't tell me what a lie is, damn it! I've been in your room and read all those letters she wrote you. You're not *like* me; we look so *different*. Christ sake . . . !"

"You read my letters?"

"Yes. I found the Goddamned hiding place where you keep your Goddamned treasures—those filthy lies . . . you don't belong with me. You believe that, don't you?"

"Should I? Are they lies? Do I belong with you?"

"Yes. You belong with me. One more word out of you, and I'll paste that loose mouth of yours. And just for the record, I'm not giving you a dime for that trip to New York."

Robert buckled slightly, and his eyes were glazed as if he could not believe we were quite real, as if a nightmare element was here in the room, hazy like the sunshine that fell through the window, but only the nightmare was real; the three-step nightmare of Ann, and school, and the letters. "I don't care what you give me, ever." He got up, turned almost drunkenly toward the hallway.

"Where did you put my letters?"

His father smiled. "I burned them."

Motionless, they stared at each other in silence. It was like the strings had been cut that made people move. Then he dropped back onto the couch. His face was red; anguish pulled at the corners of his mouth; and I knew he was going to cry.

"Let me go!" I said.

His father looked over at me, as if he had forgotten I was there, and he seemed a little afraid. "Go on," he said.

Robert turned his face into a corner of the couch. I heard

the first sob and tore at the latch chain. As it gave way, I looked back: Paul, his red hair tousled, was looking up at his father, mouth quivering.

"Are you mad at me, too, Daddy?"

"Of course not, son," Mr. Garrety said.

I went out. I heard Robert shout, and then heavy rushing footsteps over the carpet—then no more. I was away. Why? I asked myself. Why did I always want to run? I should have been running now, but I should not have wanted to run so much. Even at home I ran from discord, and if I could not run, I slipped into a dream. Why? What did I have to fear? What terrible things would happen to me? I did not know. But I was afraid of what I could not dream my way through, refract through a rosy cloud. I sought all my solutions in dreams; dreamed my way in and around a situation, drawing back when it got too hot for me, hitting out when I sensed a thrust, covering myself with sarcasm, abusive humor, the let-up of wild, confused laughter; hitting, hitting, hitting through a growing intoxicant until even the simplest people and institutions were fair objects. I ran when I could not hit. When I hit I ran, too. I did not want to run any more.

When I reached my home twenty minutes later, I could still see it in my mind, Robert, his father, his brother, staring wildly at each other, and I could hear the mystery of their shouts and heavy rushing footsteps. I trembled. I began to see him as me, turning into action things I dreamed of. I went to my room and started to read a book, then discarded it and paced around, turning myself into Robert, hitting the father, saying something eloquent, and I did not know what then. What could I do, or he do? What was there to do? When the thing you wanted most was refused, and the girl you loved and the school you attended, kicked you out? I could not say to myself that this could not happen to me, I'm not that stupid to cause all those things, so it doesn't concern me, because I knew how easily it had happened.

It was three-thirty, and I had been home an hour and a half when he phoned.

15

"Meet me," he said in a deep voice.

"Why? What happened?"

"I can't tell you now. I'll be in Norman's drugstore at Santa Monica and Hillcrest. Keep quiet about it."

"Okay. So long."

It was past four when I reached the drugstore. He was sitting at the counter, and he looked pale. I sat down on the stool next to his and watched him in the long mirror directly opposite. Apparently I wasn't going to receive any acknowledgment until the few people around us had left. In the mirror his face was like a stranger's who bore his resemblance: I realized something had changed, something really characteristic had entered his face since our last semester at school. It was not merely that he had grown, so that he stood two inches over the middle height already, or that he seemed stronger or that he seemed to handle himself, if not with more confidence, at least more methodically, but his face seemed thinner, gaunt, as if to emphasize the separate features. He was better-looking and older-looking; his nose was straight, long and noble-looking, and his eyes, large and dark brown, almost dominated the face. He looked easily seventeen, but he still had six months before he became fifteen.

The people moved off, and we became more or less alone.

He turned then and smiled. "How're you doin', Jack?"

He sounded authoritative suddenly. I shrugged. "What's coming off?"

"I've got twenty-five dollars. Do you want to see it?"

"I'll believe you."

"It's from my bank account set up by some decrepit uncle. It used to be fifty dollars, but I kept withdrawing from it until complaints were thrown by parents. Anyway, it's busted now."

I was a little disappointed after his urgent phone conversation. "Tell me what happened after I left, will you?"

He lit a cigarette, and glanced around at the front and back entrance of the drugstore. "After you ran, I said to my brother, 'Get out!' and untrue threw a fit, so I went to my room. I was *slightly* feeling shame; it wouldn't have been so bad if you weren't there. And steppy screamed for me to come out. And little brother was crying, and untrue father said, 'I'm getting out of this house. When I come back I don't want to see you here, Robert, unless you can apologize.' I'm just beaten everywhere. So I rushed. I'm taking off."

I thought a minute. "When're you coming back?"

"Never."

"But you have to." It suddenly dawned on me with a jolt that he was running away.

"Why?"

"You have to, that's all!"

"Why don't you come along?"

I thought a minute, ordered coffee, and waited until the waitress went away. "No," I said.

"What's here? Come with me!"

I thought of forests climbing mountainsides, wild, swirling blue skies, a brook in a valley far below riding the sun on its back; new cities, summer springing out of the land. "I don't want to be running." I did not want to run from anything any more. Yet I was for him, he was *me;* my better half refused to leave, but I also wanted him to succeed. "Where will you go?"

"My mother, naturally."

"Hitchhiking?"

"Naturally." He looked down at his cold coffee. "I don't want you to think I just had a thousand inspirations. I didn't up and think, 'Oh, I'm leaving.' Of course I didn't plan it for today. It just happened all at once and I knew what to do, that's all."

"Yeah. But you'll come back?"

"Oh, why don't you come with me? Then you'll know whether I'm coming back or not."

"Because I can't. Forget it."

"What's preventing it?"

"One of us has to stay. You just pretend I'm there."

He tasted his coffee and made a face. "I wonder what new fits untrue will throw when I see my mother and she tells me who my father really is."

"Hell, I wish you didn't have to go."

"So do I! Do you think I'm overjoyed and all depressions are crushed? No, sorry! Beaten."

"Think they've called the cops by now?"

"They've probably noticed the emptiness of my room and

their fingers are crossed. But that reminds me I can't stay here much longer because if they did catch me, it wouldn't be so hot, would it? Not that they will—but a thousand precautions."

"I see, RobGarMerCom."

"Shake, JacClarApTan!"

We laughed.

"Hell, we didn't have such bad times, did we?"

He reached in his pocket and paid the bill. "No. We Prince-Johnned everywhere and girls were fainting and I charged and merry-making was evident."

"And there were attempts to end the friendship by others."

"Ha! The jealousies because they couldn't also suede. And we partnered on the hideous ones, the jolly giant and the blond strength, and we were beaten but we also beat them and a hump was thrown, and Ann was weeping and then I was beaten, but maybe she will have a child by me, and I will laugh."

"As your throat is being slit by dozens of people."

"Uh!" he mocked me. "But be sure to terrorize Danni while I'm gone and drink her champagne. And advance on all the girls at Chi-ro, and terrorize Carol and make her scream and then rush at Kathy and say, 'Oh, the shortness is beating me,' and make the granny mix scotch. And then suede over to Debbie's house with the ermine draped on the sidewalk and be smoking Lord's."

"Wonder what happened to Debbie?"

"Oh, she and Ann have probably gotten together again and they're saying, 'Oh, men, how hideous! Back to each other!' "

I roared, and my laughter ran up and down inside and

made me shake. But now he was looking long and hard through the window at a brown-suited man with crew-cut blond hair who was about to cross the street. I touched his shoulder. "That's a juvie," he said.

"How do you know?"

"He took care of us after that car wreck. My mother's new Buick. Remember?"

The juvie was crossing over to the back entrance.

"I'm going," he said, jerking to his feet. "My father could have called the cops after all!"

"Take it easy!"

"So long!" He darted out the front door, I saw him through the side window hurrying down the sidewalk and then he was lost in the crowd.

The man came down the counter slowly. I was aware only of the brown suit, I did not dare look back at his face. He tapped me on the shoulder.

"Let's see your ID."

I took out my wallet and handed it to him with a scared feeling.

The first thing he saw was my student body membership, and that was enough to make him return the wallet. "C'mon."

He put his hand on my arm, and we walked side by side up the back corridor and half a block down the street to a waiting prowl car. "Get in." I sat down in the back seat and he moved alongside me. His partner sat in front casually watching us through the rearview mirror.

"My name's Sergeant Johnson, Jack," the brown-suited man said. "Where do you live?"

I told him.

"We're going for a little ride."

"How come?"

"You'll see."

We drove about eight blocks to a small, wood-frame house where the driver, leaning on his horn, drew out of the front door an old man in a tattered blue shirt and a wrinkled chin covered with white and gray bristles.

"He the one?" Sergeant Johnson asked.

I was relieved it wasn't about Robert.

The old man squinted at me. I smiled. It was all ridiculous.

"No, no," he said, "much younger fella, punier fella." He talked with the officers a little further, then went back inside.

"Just checking you out," Sergeant Johnson told me.

"What happened?"

There was silence.

"His daughter was raped," the driver said.

I didn't know whether to believe him or not. But I saw him smiling superciliously in the rearview mirror. "Anyway, can I go now?"

"We'll drive you back to where we picked you up," Sergeant Johnson said. "But—uh . . . roll up your sleeves."

I rolled them up, he acquitted me, and five minutes later I was standing in front of the drugstore again. I was keyed up, knifed by feelings of happiness and relief mixed with disappointment and nostalgia. I had walked almost half the long way home before I even realized it.

16

Robert's father phoned me around dinner-time and asked if Robert was with me, and when I said no, if I knew where Robert could be. I said I didn't know that either. He thanked me, and hung up.

Two days later, when I returned from school, there was a message to call him. When I did, he asked if I had seen or heard from Robert at all since yesterday. His voice carried a deeper, almost desperate ring of concern now.

"If you do see him, tell him to phone home at once—it's very important. Please." And he added, "I really don't know where he is. No one knows."

I was sorry. I really didn't know either. It made me think.

But it was different at Chi-ro—a great sensation; an eager bunch of us told what we knew. I said vaguely I had been the last to see him, but it turned out that a girl had spotted him later, on a bus going down Wilshire; he had been looking intently at the landscape, his face pale, and returned her wave with a blank stare. She had been standing at the foot of Westwood Boulevard.

I had thought he was taking off as fast as he could and

wasn't about to halt along the way, but I was wrong. A boy who lived in Santa Monica had seen him in the park on the cliffs that overlook the ocean and the coast highway, leaning on one of the cannons like he was meditating. The boy was passing by in a car and shouted out to him, but he didn't think Robert heard.

After that, there was nothing. No words, no glimpses, and in the days that followed rumors filled the vacuum.

He was in Bakersfield working on a farm . . . he had joined the Navy . . . he was wandering around Chicago attracted by gangsters. Others were more romantic: that I had him hidden in my house, that I knew where he was and I was bringing food to him, that Ann knew where he was and she was bringing love to him, that he had written Ann a long letter and she would never tell.

I knew where he was going, but I did not say it; I kept it to myself because he would have wanted me to. He had always wanted to be thought of as rather fabulous, "the glorious one," and the wild, romantic rumors would have excited him. But I knew he would never seem the same to the others. His reputation was set. Or finished.

Life grew paler but more safe. I thought about him often, and sometimes in the mornings I wondered if I shouldn't see him coming up the front walk, enhanced by some marvelous change.

The Saturday after he left I went down to the beach for the first time after the winter and saw Kathy. I went straight up to her, without any hesitation, a little dizzy with the heat and badly sunburned, and she met my eyes with astonishment. She was overwhelming. Her thighs swam up into her suit, and her hips bent into a voluptuously slender waist, her torso was stately, her skin rich with a delicate tan. I had a beer in me and had been attempting to play football in the heavy, sluggish sand; I had seen her while stumbling in the ocean with a sodden towel around my shoulders. Thinking about her face so often my impression of it had been worn down, and now I discovered hazel-brown eyes, non-penetrating but not impenetrable, not seeking as Debbie's had, not longing, and I suddenly knew that was what had always attracted me: the non-comprehension, the look that concealed nothing, did not ask and did not give. I wanted that mystery. She had sculptured features. Her nose made a kind of renaissance profile, and her skin was very clear and smooth.

Before she could break away to join her friends inside the club to which I did not belong, I said, in an off-hand way, I loved her. My best friend was gone and how sad that she should desert me, too. Like casually opening a door and being greeted by something that was both frightening and fascinating, when she realized what I was saying, she could hardly speak; but I could see, too, she was flattered as once Ann had been flattered when she discovered how Robert felt about her. She had something she could play with, something she could work around in her mind according to her will, and I was going to allow any length of time to make a decision. I felt as if a load had passed from me; I had lifted it from my heart and given it to her, and whether she kept it or not, at least I was free of it. But there were other things on my mind besides our meeting.

It had been late Friday afternoon, a week after Robert ran away, when his father came to my house. His face was pale, the skin almost blue around the eyes, and veins visible on his lids. He spoke with my mother for five minutes, his voice a little hoarse, then asked if he could see me alone. There was a glowering sky, and he had come in with a trench coat over his arm. "Out in my car," he said.

I had wondered if he would start threatening me but as we came down the walk, he was reserved. We got into the front seat, and for a long time said nothing; I looked down at my hands. When he offered me a cigarette, I accepted. As I took a light, he said: "Let's be friends, Jack. And let's be honest."

"All right."

"Do you know where he's gone?"

Suddenly I wanted to help him. "He said something about his mother."

"Oh, I thought of that, too. First thing." He lit a cigarette for himself and I stared at the soft rain outside. "I've phoned her twice. Asked her to call me at once if he contacts her. I wonder if she really will."

"That's all I know," I said. "Looks like I can't help you, Mr. Garrety."

"But maybe you can. Maybe you can tell me what's setting him off to—do these wild things."

Yes, maybe I could; but I didn't dare. How could I say it in words, when even Robert was afraid to say it to him?

"He's not even half grown up," his voice went on. "He's—did he ever tell you?"

"Fourteen."

"Fourteen—and he's got a lot to learn. Realize what he's up against?"

"I don't know."

"Tramps, bums, hunger, rain . . ." He gazed out the window. "What a hell of a kid. If only he'd let me know, say he was all right, he wouldn't even have to come back. But what is he doing? Where is he?"

The rain fell a little harder. I threw out my cigarette and rolled up the window. We weren't having a discussion any more; he was telling me things he needed to say to someone, the things he was afraid of; the only way I could help him was by listening.

"He never knew when he had it good," he said. "When he had a good home, when he was going to a good school, when he had a woman who was willing to be his mother and love him and take care of him. Maybe he knows now. A hell of a kid, and he said one marriage wasn't good enough for me. You were there and you heard him say it."

"Uh-huh."

"It's hard for a man alone to raise a small boy. I kept him in a boarding home for a while, then there were housekeepers . . . Legally, we shared his custody, his mother and I, but when it came her turn, she was always going out of town with a road show or rehearsing for something, and when she did take him, it wasn't so good. Half the time she'd forget to feed him—leave him alone. He doesn't remember that, of course. He was too young. When I met Jacqueline and finally married her—well, it was a blessing—for him. He should thank his stars I had guts enough to marry again. Maybe that's what I should've said to him."

It was painful to be here now. I wanted to leave.

"I never tried to turn him against his mother." He stared fixedly out the driver's window, away from me, cigarette slanted in his mouth. "I could have very easily. But I didn't. He thinks she's next to a saint, and when I say anything against her, it sounds like sacrilege."

"I suppose."

"That was a mistake, and burning the letters was a mistake. But when I read them it made me sore. I took the worst—the ones where she tore into me and Jacqueline, and threw them in the fire. I left the others."

"I see."

"Doing what I had never done before—creating hate."

"He doesn't hate you."

He put out his cigarette and lit another. I was getting cold. "He shouldn't. I wish I *had* sent him to his mother. Then he would have seen. But she wouldn't let me."

"What do you mean?"

"Never let me. I *could* have sent him last Christmas—but she told me he'd be inconvenient. He'd still have blamed me, and I didn't see much point then in his being mad at both of us." He stared straight ahead, and the cigarette smoke wreathed his head and shoulders. "He's bent on something, visiting her. And I'm afraid of what she'll tell him."

"How's that?"

He didn't answer right away. "She could tell him something so that he'd probably never come back. And what will happen to him then, God knows. And God help him."

"If I ever hear from him——"

"Oh, sure," he said curtly, and I knew he was going to let me go.

"I hope he's all right."

"Sure. Take care of yourself, Jack."

"Okay, thank you." I opened the car door.

"So long now." He looked up. "Oh, is it raining?" he said.

17

It was a strange feeling to come to a party to which I had actually been invited. Mike MacKyntyre had phoned and said his girl was having a "shindig"—he was a very quaint fellow—and they were sitting around talking and they suddenly thought, why not invite me? I wondered if Kathy had put him up to it, but even if she hadn't, I thought I could do worse.

Mike opened the door, beaming. I saw faces so scrubbed that pinpoints of light played on the cheeks, a blur of flashing pink shoulders, the sparkle of lacquered hair. The boys wore an anonymous blue serge or charcoal. Hands slapped me on the back, now and then voices buzzed in my ear. I knew hardly anybody there, and their politeness was embarrassing. I wasn't dressed right, either. I wore a sports jacket too tight around the shoulders and blue slacks with a dull, mysterious spot on the knee. I was unaccustomed to dressing up and hadn't asked what to wear. The punch was flat and the sandwiches were stale, the bread cunningly shorn off at the heel, and the Spanish peanuts rumbled in my stomach.

Soon I had to go on a little mission, and confusing directions, opened the wrong door. Inside I saw three adults, the parents of the hostess and an older man, possibly a grandfather, staring at each other. They turned their heads at me and smiled in silence. I mumbled, "Mistake." The smiles slipped back into their mouths, they grew a little agonized and then went back to staring at each other as I shut the door.

Before I got back to the living room, Mac collared me.

"I'm sorry she hasn't come yet," he said, letting it sound unimportant.

"Who?"

"Somebody who wants to see you."

"Who the hell wants to see me?"

"She does."

My heart beat. "Who do you mean?"

"Ann."

"Oh, hell. Why does *she* want to see me?"

"I think I know." He lit a cigarette dramatically.

"I thought cigarettes'd kill you."

"I'm cured."

"Oh."

"Let's go outside." He pushed open a screen door and I followed him out to a flagstone patio. It was a long, narrow yard; about three-fourths back stood an arching trellis, thick with vines, that formed an arbor on two sides and left the middle area open to walk further on. Beyond the trellis, at the end of the property, I could see a small back gate, and in the twin arbors, stone-white, granite benches. Bright moonlight splashed through the warm air, and clouds in the sky, like beaten snow on black spring torrents, made the night even lighter.

We crossed over to the trellis, but he stopped short of going under it and nodded meaningfully. "You can wait here."

"What the hell is this?"

"She wants to talk to you."

"About what?"

"Your friend Robert. And I'm curious, too. Tell me everything."

"Tell you what? He took off. What about it?"

"I hear he got in a hold-up."

"No!"

"That's what I heard."

"From who?"

"Well—some guy who heard it from someone else."

"You can tell him it's a lie. He left because there's something he has to do, that's all."

Mac dropped the cigarette on the wet grass. "Did he talk about me?"

"When do you mean?"

"The day he left. Did I have something to do with it?"

"You had nothing to do with it. He never thought about you."

"Oh." He was mad at me. He was very vain, and I had an idea he had been the one to start the rumor about the hold-up. "Well, anyway, why don't you stay here behind the trellis; she'll be along in a few minutes."

"Can't I come back to the party?"

"Wait at least a few minutes." He cut across the lawn and went back inside the house. I cursed him and sat down to wait on the stone bench. Being invited was not much better than crashing the place. I thought about Robert, and the sullen, frightened look he'd had in the drugstore before he walked out and then his angry eyes, his fierce gestures. It seemed a long, long time ago, a party past, a conscience past, and scenes, feelings, and many thoughts. There was more between him and me than mere time; it was already the past, I was already remembering. He had jaded me on seeking the close friendship of others. We had communicated too much; I did not ever want to communicate so much again. I saw us again, tormented and tormenting, our sides aching from laughter.

I heard light footsteps and got up. Ann halted just outside the arbor, looked at me in appraisal. Light from the party shone behind her face, and thrown in shadow it was pretty and soft and her eyes were radiant. She was wearing a pink organdy gown with a gauzy wrap around that spread out from the edge of her pink shoulders. Her blond hair was thick, streaked, and healthy-looking, and fluffed up from the nape of her neck. I remembered her in the coffee shop that last time, her hesitant hand on the door knob, the way she sat stiffly with wet blue eyes, and then her voice: "You really aren't going to bother me again, are you?"

And suddenly I wasn't angry any more. "I was told to wait," I said. "You look—very nice. Very."

She hesitated but drew forward. "This may seem strange—having you meet me here, I mean. I can't stay long." She sat down on the bench. "I came to talk about him."

"I know."

"You're his best friend, aren't you?"

"Yes."

She raised her chin; her neck muscles were taut. She was suddenly afraid, and gently I took her hand. It was a soft hand, very white; the nails were short and unpainted. She leaned against my shoulder. Her eyes were only half open.

"There's a moon out tonight."

"I see it."

"It looks cold and dirty."

I was shocked. "It's a beautiful moon, and you're pretty." I wished I had said she was beautiful, too. Then I thought about Kathy, and was glad I hadn't said it. Then I didn't know whether I was glad I had said it or not. I didn't know whether I was being stupid or noble.

"Do you miss my friend Debbie?"

"Not very much."

She turned toward me, and our cheeks touched. I shivered; her cheek was warm. She looked into my eyes with her own startled, trusting ones, and my heart pounded.

"You know him so well, don't you?"

"Yeah."

"I'm afraid."

"Don't be afraid."

"Did he—did he do it for me?"

I was surprised. "Partways."

"God."

"Yes. Partly for you. He's out there. Think about that."

She shuddered. "Lord! What could I have done?"

"Nothing."

"Does he—does he still love me?"

I looked away from her. "Hell, I don't know."

"Did he tell you?"

"He thought about you often."

"Then, he did do it because of *me*?"

She said it so positively I knew—like Mac—that was what she thought. "No, not really. For his mother. No one would let him see her. Don't tell anybody. He's probably gone to see her in New York."

"I—I was like a mother to him, supposedly?"

"Yeah."

"You're good to tell me," she said, her voice suddenly cold.

"I'm glad you think so."

"Fred's inside. I have to go back. I couldn't get rid of him for tonight. He's still mad at you."

She really wowed me. "So—what'll I do?"

"There's a back gate: I'll let you out."

We left the arbor the rear way and crossed over to the back gate. "This is a rotten deal," I said.

"Don't think that."

"What am I supposed to think?" I rested my hand on the latch; out of the corner of my eye I saw her glancing back at the house. "Now you got your information you're kicking me out, aren't you?"

"Would you rather it was me or Fred?"

"That isn't the point."

She motioned me to hurry. "Why don't you just get out anyway! C'mon! We'll discuss it sometime."

"I'll go when I feel like it."

"I'll get Fred," she answered. "Is that what you want?"

"Why didn't you get him ten minutes ago?" I heard a couple coming out to the patio, but no longer cared about anyone raising an alarm; I did not want to be running again. "Listen, do you know what you can do? You can run around screaming and making threats, but I'm not going to move—because that's the only thing you want from me now, and I wouldn't give it to you for anything."

"Oh, is that right?" she demanded. "Well, if you *think*

you're staying, you've got another thought coming. I had you invited here in the first place, and now I'm asking you to get out. I don't want anything more to do with you either."

"Just a little something to do with my best friend when you feel like it."

She raised her hand to slap me but I caught her wrist.

"Let go!" she cried.

I heard people coming out the door. I expected her to grapple with me, and really thought we were of equal strength, but she twisted her arm with frantic helplessness, fearing for her dress, and tears came in her eyes.

I let go.

"Hey, I'm sorry, Ann," I said. "I thought you were so strong——"

"You thought I was what?"

"I wouldn't have held you that hard. We always thought you were so strong. Don't cry now," I said weakly. "I didn't hurt you. Don't cry, for God's sakes."

"Leave me alone. Get out!"

A crowd was running toward the trellis, and with it I thought I saw Fred.

"What's going on?" MacKyntyre shouted.

"You ought to know," I shouted back, "you planned it!"

Tall and formidable, Fred pushed Mac out of the way and drew toward us. The crowd came rushing in back of him.

Ann shoved me against the gate. She was scowling, and her voice was grating and rapid. "I never want to hear his name again. I hate him. I hate Robert. Get out and leave me alone. Leave me alone!"

Fred came between us, like a teacher separating two pupils,

angry, very pale. "What the hell're you d-doing?" he stuttered.

"None of your Goddamn business," I said, my knees shaking. "But Ann, don't ever try to use me to build up your stinking vanity——"

"You bastard!" she hissed.

Fred stared at her.

"Maybe you were all right before," I said, "but the second you asked if he did it for you, because knowing would be kicks, that made you a tramp——"

"Get out of here," Fred half whispered.

"Bastard!" she said again.

I breathed heavily. The crowd's judgment of who was right or wrong was going against me. "That's what the kid will be, yours and Robert's—if you have it."

There was a hush, and no one seemed to move.

Tears sprang in her eyes—everything else had gone out—she came at me like a witch—her hands raised as though to claw my cheeks, and then suddenly her face contorted as if she had been lashed from side to side, and she burst into a sob. "Get out!" she said in a terrifying voice.

Somebody in high heels, perhaps one of the trapped parents who wondered where the party had migrated, opened the door to the patio and stepped outside.

"Children? Children?" she inquired.

We looked up, we did not answer. The secret was already frozen in us and the misty, detached voice would never know it, would never suspect.

"Get out of here," Fred whispered. "For Christ's sake get out of here!"

"God, don't I want to get out here, don't I want to get you

out of my life—all of you—and forget all about you. God, isn't that what I want over anything!" I went out; no one spoke; I could hear Ann drawing heavy breath from her sobs. I could feel the tension, I breathed it in and out; they had judged me in the right, and they wanted to mob me for it. The woman kept calling for the children. I walked slowly at first, then faster, and then I began to run.

I ran faster than I had ever run before, and I did not know where I was going. Houses became black streaks of light, my eyes jiggled, and something seemed to be pressing down on the top line of my vision. Blocks went by, my lungs drew pain, my mouth was parched, and my legs were unconnected groups of muscles running much too fast, so that, when I slowed finally, they almost collapsed and I had to sit down on the curb of a street. I tried very hard, but for the time being I could not get up. It caught me, it had always been on my heels, and I took my head in my hands and shook and cried. I felt sorry for what I had done because we shouldn't have deserved it, neither her nor me, and Robert shouldn't have, either. It wasn't nice out in the world like I used to think, and people weren't as nice as they really liked to be in their hearts.

18

The following Friday Robert had been gone three weeks. Only five days of school remained, and I was in my room studying for final exams when I heard the phone ring.

"Jack, it's for you," my mother called out.

I went to her room and took up the receiver. "Hello?"

"Jack!"

It was Robert. "Wait a minute," I said hurriedly. I drew the phone out into the hallway and shut the door. "When'd you get back?"

"About twenty minutes ago. Meet me."

"Where are you?"

"L.A. Bus terminal."

"I'll be right down! Hey!"

"What?"

"Do your parents know you're here?"

"No."

"Have you been to New York?"

"Yes!"

Excitement and astonishment flowed into me in tremendous waves. Suddenly I felt he was really here! "Where do I meet you?"

"I'll be around the orange juice counter."

"Okay. Good-by!"

I told my mother I was going to meet somebody up in Hollywood and ran out of the house.

It took me forty minutes to hitchhike down to the terminal. I went inside and circled the lobby looking for the orange drink stand; it stood at the far end, almost deserted. But it was not until I came up to the counter that I spotted him sitting on a bench between two concessions booths, glancing in the opposite direction with a folded newspaper in his hand. He was pale and haggard and he had gotten a butch; the clothes he wore were the same, now wrinkled and dusty, but his half boots were neatly polished.

"Robert! Hey!"

He got up, and his eyes sparkled as though by seeing me he knew he was really home. "How are you?" he said, grabbing my hand.

I smiled. "Excited. So what goes?"

"Oh, it was tremendous. Hideous in a way."

We sat down on the bench and lit cigarettes. I cuffed him.

"What's going on?" he asked.

"Nothing," I said. "Your father came to see me, and he was sad. Last week I went to a party and saw Ann and beat her because she's a tramp . . ." I told him exactly what had happened.

He scowled, but said nothing.

"Now it's your turn. I want to hear all about what you did."

He leaned back against the wall. People passed to and fro across the lobby, but in the recess between the two stands we remained out of earshot. "What do you want to hear about?"

"Everything! For God's sakes, you know I want to hear about everything!"

He rubbed his eyes slowly, and yawned. "The first night I hitchhiked up to San Francisco."

"How'd you like it?"

"I don't know. I didn't stay very long." He sighed and crossed his legs at the knee. "I hate cross-country buses. I'm never going to ride in one again . . . After San Francisco I went over to Oakland and I picked up some girl and she was a limp."

"Huh?"

"I mean, I didn't know it until I followed her off the street car into some Tuleville spot. She was in an accident and she couldn't walk hardly. So I asked her to marry me."

"You asked her to marry you?"

"And she was a limp. And then I went to Sacramento and then to Truckee—God, it was so cold at night—and the next day I covered Nevada and it was hot as hell. And the next night I walked and walked and walked outside this little town called Wendover in Utah and I nearly died but I finally got back to the town and in a motel and slept . . . It was the only time I slept in a bed for ten days."

"You had bad times then?"

"Once outside Salt Lake City I got panicked and destroyed all my ID and that was the night the cops were looking for an escaped convict, and so three different times they beat me with a thousand questions. I had to walk on a mountain road with some other hitchhiker and stay on the dividing line so I wouldn't get shot, and it was freezing. And that lasted all night long. But it wasn't so bad as some other times because I had somebody with me."

"It wasn't?"

"No. Like the next night I was outside Denver and I just kept on walking and walking and it got night and nobody would pick me up because in Colorado they can jail you for hitchhiking. I walked nineteen miles and I had had it and I could have died and it was like it wouldn't have mattered to me. And I slept in the high grass next to the wheat fields and I was afraid . . . And you know one thing that still makes me afraid? Even on the bus? All the stars in the sky the way they are in the mountains in Utah. It was so cold there nothing moved and you couldn't see out at all, you couldn't see the hand in front of your face. Just the stars. And it's like you die. You look up and your neck gets numb because you keep bending back and you feel like you're not living any more, and your soul watches."

"Sounds like hell."

"And Topeka—oh, outside Topeka all these little hills and the wind rushing at you and God, you can't see. It was that dark, I mean I can't tell you how dark. It was black-dark, like it lived. And once I got caught in brambles and I was bleeding, and then once I went under a bridge to sleep and someone got after me and I never saw his face and I ran. And I couldn't go to sleep anywhere, I wasn't safe anywhere. And dawn came and I found a drainage pipe along the ground and I climbed in and it was warm there and as I went off to sleep, I saw a spider over my head and I didn't even kill it." He had drawn forward, nervous and tense, but now he leaned back against the wall again, and lit another cigarette. "Later I got a ride to St. Louis, and the next morning after that I was in Pittsburgh. It was raining and I didn't get to Philadelphia till midnight. Those nights and days weren't so bad."

"What happened in New York City?"

"I had to walk about thirty blocks to my mother's apartment. As I walked in there was slight shock on her face, and my other father was there scowling and he acted like he thought I was up to something, but he finally left us alone."

"And you asked her?"

"No."

"You didn't even ask her?"

"No, Jack, it's this way: she wouldn't know." Tears came in his eyes, and he looked straight ahead, across the long, crowded lobby. "Because that's the way it is with her. She wouldn't know! She wouldn't *know*. And why ask? It doesn't matter the way it is."

"But, my God——"

"Listen, I'll tell you something if you'll promise you'll never tell it to anybody else. My mother said before she was married to my father he used to charge at her frantically but he was unliked. They got married during some crazy graduation summer, and after a little while they were hating each other and he was always checking up on her and showing jealousy. So she ran to New York, but he hunted her down and pleaded with her on his knees—and she went back to him and that lasted another two years. Then she ran out again—first she told me he threw her out, then she said she left— I was eighteen months old by this time, and he took care of me. She said there was a tremendous battle over me when I was four or five years old."

"In court?"

"Yes. So she says because of him she isn't a big star. She was only mixed up with him for three years, but she blames him. Also me. Because inches were thrown around the waist as I was born and many jobs were lost when she was young. I bet."

"Maybe he is your father after all."

"It doesn't matter. Because all this about their married life got me to thinking that my admiration for Ann was like my father beating my mother endlessly as he was hated. And I knew I was like my father—and I didn't care about a minor thing like blood."

"Oh. But what was your mother like?"

"At first she was running around and asking if I was content. Then we went out to eat and she met friends, and the embarrassment because I was ages, and a thousand shocks as the huge son is seen. She told everybody she was married when she was sixteen, and after we'd gotten out of the restaurant she said she was going to buy me a suit so she'd be proud of me. So we bought a ready-made suit, and I strode around with her and she kept showing me off. I was a novelty to her."

"Well, what happened afterwards?"

"Afterwards all these co-actors came to the apartment, and the ones who weren't working kept bringing people down. And the next day my mother had coke for breakfast. I don't know why. She said it was from the days when she was poor. Then, at dinner, martinis. And all the time the husband—he works in some office—and the little girl is always being sent to the grandmother."

"Did she finally send you home?"

"Oh no. She wanted me to stay because I was a novelty, and I was all grown-up, so she wouldn't have to bother much over me. But I decided to go back. You might say I ran away from her, too. I schemed bus fare from her; she never even saw me off. I left the suit behind because I didn't think she'd want me to have it here."

"Why didn't she phone your father?"

"I said I'd phone. She couldn't care less." His eyes fell shut.

"Well, what about your father? How do you feel about him?"

"Why don't you look at it this way: he's an untrue father, I'm an untrue son, right? So if it's bad for me, it's *worse* for him." He bent his head toward his shoulder, and dozed a little.

"When're you going home?"

"Never," he murmured. He opened his eyes. "Stay with me, will you?"

Then he fell asleep.

I shook his shoulder. "You can't go to sleep here! Wake up! Wake up!"

He shook his head. "I haven't slept for five days!"

"Let's bum up to your house."

"No!"

"Why?"

He scowled at me a minute. "Oh, I don't know."

I shrugged. "Give me a reason."

"Well, I want to go back . . ."

"He wants you back!"

"He does? . . . Oh, so what."

"You can't exist in a bus terminal."

"I can exist in any damn place in the country—that's one thing I found out."

"But if the cops pick you up and bring you home it won't be very glorious."

"You're right!" he said. "I didn't think about that. It would be very hideous, wouldn't it?"

"Get up."

"But this isn't right. I just can't walk in and say 'Hello.' I have to suede, so they'll know I didn't get drunk or something and decided to leave for a little while to crawl back. No! *Sorry.*" He rose. "Never crawl because nothing is worth crawling to."

"What are you planning on doing?"

"I don't know but something spectacular so the triumphs will be gleaming, and they'll say, 'Oh, we are humbled, he's come and he'll be a good boy now.'"

He might have thought it was all right, but I could anticipate a wild arrival with Robert falling asleep five minutes later, helpless to quiet the atmosphere, and me being questioned for several hysterical hours. But on the other hand if Robert did not go home immediately, I could see ourselves wandering up and down residential streets at two o'clock in the morning; or if he was passed out by then, me sitting guard over his sleeping body. I guessed, too, if he did not go home immediately, there would be emotional complications with his parents when they found out. So I decided on a definite plan before we even got outside the terminal.

"We better take the bus," I said.

"I hate buses! I just rode three thousand miles in one!"

"Then we'll take a taxi. How much money you got?"

"Three dollars."

"That's about what it should take. So you'll be coming back

independent—you hold out a buck and let me make up the full amount." It was half of my allowance.

He never asked me where we were going; when we were about twelve blocks from the terminal, he fell asleep again, and I decided not to wake him.

We got out several blocks from his house, with everything deserted. He squinted up the dark, quiet street. "Where am I?"

"Almost home."

He woke up suddenly. "I told you I wasn't going home yet."

"Oh, I got a spectacular thing planned."

"What?"

"Just c'mon."

He staggered up the sidewalk, veering right, then left a little, like a drunk. Under the street lights I could see he was even more pale. His hands quivered, and he scowled continually.

"How far, Jack?"

"Three blocks."

"Are you with me, Jack?"

"I'm with you."

"Where are you?" He laughed uproariously. "You should've seen those plains outside Denver. God, they were big, Jack. You can't stop, can't stop a minute. You gotta keep going, Jack."

"You're crazy."

He shivered. "Look at the stars, Jack. Like Utah. They make you afraid . . . so still. It isn't very cold tonight."

"No."

"Are we nearly there?"

"Oh, almost."

"I proved myself, didn't I?"

"I guess."

"Just because I'm the illegitimate one . . . being thrown at doorsteps with the orphanages informed. That don't mean I can't do mighty things like walking the plains and nearly dying and charging hundreds of women."

"No."

"Is it very much farther? I'm so tired I can't even tell."

"Not much."

"You should have seen the forests, Jack, all the forests I went through. And deer watching through the leaves, and sometimes off the highway these streams bubbling around, but I could never stop long and I only skipped stones off the water. *Soda Pop Creek*. That was the true name of one. I would've called it *Liquid Ermine*."

"Sensational."

"Hey!" he grabbed my arm.

We were four houses from his. It looked silent and lonely, sheltering. "My plan is," I said, "you climb in the window of your room and lock the door and go to bed. Then next morning when they're having breakfast you stride out."

"Good! It fits me, and ermine will drape as I rush in in the morning."

We cut across the lawns of the other houses and slipped around the side of his until we reached his bedroom window. It was already open a crack. He jimmied the screen, then carefully raised the window halfway, and started to climb inside. When he had almost swung his whole body in, his foot struck a small bedside table and it pitched over to the floor with a crash and sent a lamp flying. He remained in the window half in and half out, but drew his hand back quickly in reaction and hit the screen. Grating past his skin, it unhinged from its upper screws and dropped to the ground.

"Ow!"

It struck the cement walk on end, and I jumped away.

"Get me down!" Robert said.

I went to take his hand and just then I heard his father shouting to his wife from the next room. I jerked the hand, but he hadn't ducked his head back under the window yet and struck it.

"Goddamn!"

I heard somebody cry "Eeee" next door; and suddenly the door to Robert's room opened and the light flashed on. I saw Mr. Garrety standing in the doorway with Robert's .22 rifle. From the living room came the sound of his wife dialing on the phone.

Robert smiled faintly. "I just got in—Dad."

I decided I had better get the hell out.

But it seemed to me something had slipped away, drifted out in the night never to come back again: a little world of freedom and confinement in which love, sadness, and joy broke against lonely beaches in overpowering waves. There had been too much to laugh at that was not really funny, and too much sorrow that was not even faintly sad. It was summer again, the leaves would be fresh and bright on the trees, the skies pale and hot, and the scents of licorice and rose thick in the air and maybe, for me, there would be Kathy. We had wakened from a long dream to see it was true, but dreaming had been a truth, and a reality by itself.